## PROGRAMMED FOR DEATH

Caught in a half-dozen flashlight beams, the advancing horde of three-foot-high, eight-legged walking robot bombs from the twentieth century approached the Freefighters. They beeped happily, their atomic-cell batteries feeding them power to move their sharp clawlike legs. They had found victims at last.

"Everybody run!" Rockson shouted. But the minute the Freefighters took off, the insidious metal things took off after them, like voracious insects that had spotted red meat.

Rockson, concerned for the others, should have paid more attention to his own bootheels. A scabie-bomb was suddenly on him, grabbing hold of his left boot. It was beeping faster and faster. *It was going to explode!*

## DOOMSDAY WARRIOR
### by Ryder Stacy

After the nuclear devastation of World War III, America is no more than a brutalized colony of the Soviet master. But only until Ted Rockson, soldier of survival, leads a rebellion against the hated conquerers . . .

# DOOMSDAY WARRIOR

## #11 AMERICAN EDEN

### BY RYDER STACY

**ZEBRA BOOKS**
**KENSINGTON PUBLISHING CORP.**

ZEBRA BOOKS

are published by

Kensington Publishing Corp.
475 Park Avenue South
New York, NY 10016

First printing: June 1987

Printed in the United States of America

# Prologue

December 29th:

A lone figure, hunched down against the howling winter wind, moved step by frozen step through the Colorado wilderness. He was ill clad for such a winter trek, wearing soft thin boots and a clinging mauve with-sparkles tunic. His only defenses against the cold were an engineer's cap on his platinum-blond thin hair and a scarf made of an old piece of furniture fabric wrapped several times around his thin pale neck.

The wanderer was nearly frozen to death, his cracked and bleeding gloveless hands shoved into small pockets lined with tissue paper. His pale face, buried in the fabric of the scarf, was likewise a mass of cracks. His reddish albino eyes were swollen. Anyone could tell by his shaky steps that he didn't have much more left in him. He was living out the last bitter cold moments of his unfathomable life.

I am ready to die, he thought. I have seen wonders . . . I have achieved what no man of my generation has — I have lived. Lived not like a ground rat, but like

5

a human being. I have breathed real fresh air, smelled real smells, touched real plants and flowers. I will join my companions, who fell long before me, join them in the warmth of death, away from this bitter coldness.

But such a calm numbing death would not be. The wanderer would not die of the cold. His weary bones would not rest peaceful on the whiteness. No. For a stalker approached the man. A stalker of powerful sinewy presence, a slinking nightmare called the Rocky Mountain snow leopard. It was sniffing the staggering man's footprints, just a hundred yards behind. Just a mere three seconds of unbelievable feline speed and the man would be a morsel, a victual, a nourishing treat for its ravenous desire for sustenance.

The cat had caught the scent miles away — its large nostrils could do that, pick up the scent of a human-thing, home in on it like a radar-tracking robot, until it was close enough to pounce. This had been a hard winter, with few prey to feed the twelve-hundred-pound, sixteen-foot-long mutant leopard's stomach. At last, it thought, at last I will eat.

And it dug its six-toed, double-clawed feet into the snow and took off along the footprint path, determined to end its desperate hunger. In a second, coming over a small hill, it saw the prey. Not big, not a whole stomachful, but big enough. Its huge jaw, like the watery opening of a tractor's jaw, filled with rows of razor-sharp teeth, let out a growl.

The creature saw the figure stop, turn, saw the human-thing's long thin arms raised to shield itself from the roaring, snarling death approaching.

Adrenaline ran into the cat-creature's body; digestive juices poured into its gullet. Thirty feet from the man-prey it leapt high in the air, sailed out toward dinner, confident it would devour—

"*No*," gasped the man, falling back into the snow, the creature flying at him. He closed his eyes, as if it would cease to be, as if the hurtling monster would not be there if he just shut his eyes.

And then there was a loud machine-like report. The sound of a revving combustion engine? The fall of a hundred rocks down a mountain cliff? No.

Automatic weapons firing.

The creature fell just to the side of the man-prey, yellow globe-eyes open and staring at nothing in this world. Its body was riddled with grapefruit-sized evenly-spaced holes oozing blood. Explosive-bullet holes. The man lay as still as the dead thing alongside. They lay like some weird mother and child in the red-stained snow. Blood pumped weakly through the holes in the giant cat's pelt. It steamed in the below-zero air, quickly coagulating into brown muck.

Two figures in heavy winter parkas, carrying the smoking hot Liberator rifles that had done the damage to the creature, approached. They slid easily along over the two feet of snow, gliding elegantly on short steel skis. Jeffers and Blythe of the Century City patrol corps. Men who knew these mountains and the dangers they held—men equipped to deal with that danger.

Cautiously they walked up to the strangely garbed man and the creature sprawled out there on the

7

blood-speckled whiteness. They had watched a bit before coming down the slope. Making sure. The big cat hadn't stirred except for a few trembles. Nerves settling down after violent tension.

Certain that the creature wouldn't rise again to threaten, their attention shifted to the man. What the hell was he doing out here? And why was he dressed so inadequately for the weather?

"Is he dead?" Blythe asked his companion, the icy wind half whipping away his words.

Jeffers, who sometimes doubled as a medic, bent to feel the throat of the prone human, searching for a pulse in his jugular. For a second, there was nothing. Then he felt one slow weak blip of the vessel. "I think he's alive — though barely. Come on — we've got to get him inside the mountain."

# Chapter 1

"Happy New Year," everyone gathered in Century City's vast underground Lincoln Square shouted. Rona clinked her crystal champagne glass against Ted Rockson's.

"To us," Rona said, pushing her long red hair away from her forehead with her other hand, and taking a long sip.

Rockson's mismatched light blue and violet eyes flashed, and he said, "Yes, to us, and to a peaceful New Year."

The twelve-piece dance band was playing "Auld Lang Syne"; confetti and streamers flew through the semidarkness. Horns were nearly drowning out the music. A set of streamers fell and decorated the couple's hair, the white tablecloth.

Rona stood up on her long sparkle-stockinged legs and leaned over the table and kissed her lover. The redhead lingered, but shouts of "Rockson, Rockson" made her finally desist. Her hero was being called on to make a speech.

Rockson demurred, waving his hands, shaking his

9

head *no*, but to no avail. McCaughlin, the massive Freefighter who sat looking ridiculous in a white tuxedo at a nearby table with Shannon and Detroit Green and his wife, shouted. "Go ahead, Rock, speak. It's the only way to quiet them and get on with the party. Stand in the spotlight and say a few words."

Rockson put the crystal glass down on the table and rose to wild cheering, brushing confetti out of his hair. The tall bronze-skinned man with the white streak in the middle of his jet-black hair, the man the world knew as the Doomsday Warrior, strode to the stage. The spotlight changed to plain white, and focused in uncomfortably on him.

"Citizens of Century City," Rockson began, "This is the best New Year's Day we've had in decades."

Cheers.

"The Russians are—at least temporarily—vanquished; the caverns containing this great city have been restored and expanded; and Killov, the KGB madman, our greatest enemy, is dead." More cheers. "We look forward to a prosperous and victorious new year. The tide has turned. The Soviet occupation forces, not we Americans, are on the run now. So we should all enjoy ourselves. That's all I have to say."

They shouted, "More, more," but Rockson just smiled. Finally, they let Rockson sit. A loud off-key chorus of "Auld Lang Syne" began, then the ten-piece orchestra started playing a waltz. Rona pulled Rockson up to dance, and before he could object, they were out on the floor.

She was a smooth dancer; he managed. He pressed against her. Full-bosomed Rona was quite spectacular in her low-cut gold gossamer gown. He was a lucky man. And it *was* a wonderful New Year, he thought. The best in his whole life. Years of struggle against the hated Soviet occupiers of America, years of death and desperate combat, were finally bearing fruit. Perhaps the worst days of America were behind them now. He and Rona swirled with the music, sank into each other's arms.

Then Rockson caught a movement out of the corner of his eye. It was a somber, hawk-nosed man in a desperate hurry, weaving erratically across the dance floor, cutting between dancers who deferred to the intruder. "Uh oh," Rockson said, "Here comes Rath."

"Oh no." Rona knew what that could mean. The head of Intelligence Operations and Security always had work for Rockson. "Not now," she muttered, "Oh God, not now."

It *was* now. "Something has come up," old man Rath said as he reached Rockson's shoulder. "Something that can't wait until morning."

"It'll have to wait," Rockson countered. He had seen Rath go overboard about the importance of a minor matter before.

"It can't, Rock; come with me, *now*. Excuse us Rona. This is official business."

"Not on your life, Rath," Rona nearly spat out. "This is my party, this is my New Year's celebration. It's the first one Rock and I ever spent together and — You're not going to spoil it."

"Sorry, Rona," Rath said, twisting Rockson's shoulder so that he was already dragging the well-muscled man in the black tuxedo away. "Sorry," Rath shouted back as he elbowed Rockson and himself off the dance floor. Rock shouted back, "Keep my spot, Rona. I'll be right back."

Rona stamped her high-heeled shoes in anger. She walked back toward her seat. The party went on all around her. Rona sat down, dejected. Left by her man, left standing alone in the middle of the dance floor on New Year's, for God's sake. Unbelievable.

She'd finally thought she had Rock all to herself; her rival—and friend—Kim, had departed a month earlier for New Omicron City. The whole area was now snowed in. There'd been no combat for months. Rock hadn't been on a mission, and wasn't likely to be on one until the spring. The worst snowstorm on record. So Rona had thought she and Rockson would have some time together alone at last.

That was not to be. It was either Kim or Rath who spoiled her fun. Always. Which was worse? She frowned. *Rath* was worse. When Rath wanted Rock, it meant danger for the Doomsday Warrior. Kim would just make love to him—and at least she shared him with Rona, on alternate nights. But Rath, the bad-news man, had as usual come and spoiled it. Spoiled it all.

Rona poured herself a drink and downed the bubbly. She wondered if she should stay at the party at all. Why not go to her room and cry a little? She knew Rock was gone at least until morning, despite what he had said.

"No, I will have fun, I will," Rona burst out, and stood up. "What the hell, I'll get drunk. I deserve to be drunk."

She had lots of friends here, didn't she? She looked around. Ah, there. Rona walked swiftly over to the table where Shannon, the woman from Basic Research, had been seated with her date and two other Freefighters. The unconventional Shannon, Rona noted, had dyed her hair red and orange and blue in streaks. She wore a silver gown. Shannon was out with McCaughlin this New Year's. Two seats at the couple's table were empty.

"Where's Detroit and Archer? Didn't I see them at this table a moment ago?" she asked.

"Detroit," the burly seven-foot-tall McCaughlin replied, "has staggered off with Archer to put Archer to bed in that infernal conduit-tunnel home he's made down in D Section. Archer is woozy from the champagne — he can take hooch he makes himself, but the good stuff knocks him out." He laughed.

Shannon commented, "Rona, you look stunning — where's your date?"

Rona sat down and explained. Just as she finished, Dr. Schecter walked — or perhaps *gyrated* — over on his servomechanism legs. He insisted on dancing with her to show her the improvements in his replacement legs — his real legs had been blown off years ago in a battle. Schecter, the gray-haired genius that even now wore a lab coat — his eternal outfit — boasted, "Rona, I programmed my legs for the Charleston, the Twist, and the Waltz. Which will it be?"

Rockson walked to the main elevator bank with Rath, a premonition in his mutant's mind that he knew what was coming. A *mission*. And a dangerous one, judging by the prickles standing his neck hairs on end. Those hairs were infallible. They always told him when he was heading into trouble.

13

Down in the new G Section, ten levels deeper into the hewn-out Colorado mountain that was Century City, Rockson and Rath sat down at a long polished table. Rath pulled out a third chair, though no one else was in the Security room.

Someone came in. Rockson, startled, stood up, for the man that entered was a pallid gangling sort, an albino with stringy blond-white hair, pinkish large eyes, and a small mouth.

The man's clothing was like none Rockson had ever encountered before. Strange off-mauve color, with odd patterns flickering in and out of sight as he moved slowly to sit down. He seemed weak. He made no move to shake hands and introduce himself. Rock waited for an explanation from Rath as to the identity of this odd man.

Rath said, as a way of introduction, "Rockson, this is Peth Danik. He's a stranger in these parts. Our security forces found him wandering some miles south of here. He was about to be eaten by one of our more unsavory animal friends—a snow leopard. He spent two days in the hospital being treated for hypothermia and a host of other things. His eyes were nearly shot, but you know Schecter—he fixed them up pretty well. Danik's story is a strange one indeed. I want you to hear it firsthand. I believe that what he has to say impacts our security, and the security of everyone on Earth."

"Please begin," Rock requested of the stranger.

The story Danik told in a strangely intoned voice was indeed bizarre. He was, he claimed, from an unknown, completely sealed off city buried in the Mexican mountains. A place called Eden. A totally

14

contained biosphere closed off from the world since the war back in 1989.

"We of Eden, until recently, all wanted our city to be forever hidden to the surface world. After the bombs fell, after the nuclear war, we believed the world was no longer a fit place to live. We expected that it never would be livable again, ever.

"Eden is a ten-mile-long, mile-wide world unto itself. It is a total ecosystem, self-renewing, self-contained. It has a salt lake, with the microscopic creatures like diatoms and algae that a real ocean has, and it has a marshland area too. Also there is a desert-in-miniature. It is the area directly under our artificial sun—too hot to inhabit. The sun, protected by a force field, is a lithium-ion crystal that can burn for a thousand years. Not quite the same spectrum as the sun that warms the surface world. It never can be turned off. That is why there is a planetarium. Every citizen in Eden spends one night a month under the stars projected inside our planetarium. It was the belief of the constructors of Eden that mankind *needs* a little nighttime, a change from eternal sun. The planetarium is where I learned of the stars, and how to tell direction by the stars. When I came to the surface, and determined to travel north with my companions, who all perished on the journey I'm sad to say, I used the North Star to guide me.

"Eden is much bigger, but far less developed, than Century City. Our city was designed to sustain seven thousand people—and there are that number there now; the third and fourth generations of the original inhabitants."

Rockson spoke up, "You say that it is a complete

15

ecosystem—a miniature self-renewing world like the Earth, in miniature. Yet you fail to mention the terrain that on Earth helps recycle the air and water. You didn't mention rain forests. Without trees, the Earth's oxygen supply would diminish and all life would die out. In the 1980s mankind was on the verge of destroying the Amazon jungle in Brazil, where most of the Earth's atmosphere is regenerated by the trees. Then, of course, the war came, and one of its few beneficial effects was to stop the exploitation of the Amazon jungle. Do you understand what I'm getting at? A salt lake is part of an ecosystem, but how about greenery? How about trees?"

"I understand, Rockson. I omitted something: The engineers of Eden had built substitutes for trees. They made machines that mimic the properties of the rain forest—a giant filter that uses geothermal energy to strain the air of harmful waste gases and replenish it with oxygen. Plus there is some air supply available from natural caverns, deeper under the Earth. Pure cold air. And we have some plants—mostly in the marshlands adjoining our lake. Everything in Eden—or almost everything—is recycled. Carbon dioxide exhaled by the people is used by the plants—like on the rest of the Earth. They absorb the carbon dioxide from exhalation, and provide oxygen—helping our artificial means to do so. Some of the human waste was supposed to be used to feed the algae in the water and fertilize crops—but this system was never completed. We have been living on canned food and some plastic-sealed dried food."

"No crops?" Rath interjected. "Why, that's terrible. Even here in Century City—and this is a city that doesn't seal itself off—we have hydroponic gardens. Without fresh food, your health, even your ability to procreate, must suffer and—"

"Yes, it is a problem. When the—trouble—began, I proposed getting supplies of fish and seeds from the surface, so that we might eat better, but Stafford—our dictator, who I will explain about momentarily—says all things from the surface are evil, contaminated. We suffer ill health as you have stated, and breeding for us is impossible. Sex does not exist in Eden. We had our last child ten years ago. We are dying out."

# Chapter 2

Rockson was amazed by Danik's story so far. He asked, "Who created Eden? How was such a project begun back in the twentieth century? Who had that vision?"

"The money came from an American millionaire. Edward Renquist. Renquist was obsessed with the idea that World War Three was inevitable. This was because Renquist's own father perished in Hiroshima."

"Was Renquist's father Japanese?" Rath asked.

"No, his father, Johnathan, was an American POW in Hiroshima at the time the Americans nuked it—thus ending World War Two. Jonathan survived the blast—unlike most of the city's inhabitants—because the jail was a solid building on the outskirts of the city.

"The cell he was in had a hole blown in it, though. He survived by immersing himself in a cesspool, breathing through a reed. Unfortunately, he was discovered the next day by crazed survivors. Since he was an American, like those who dropped the bomb, they tortured him to death—peeled his skin off inch by inch with surgical scissors.

"Renquist was born the day his father died. He grew up to be a brilliant youth and patented many inventions from the age of twelve onward. He was always fearful, though. Mankind used atomic weapons in Japan, in 1945, and Edward Renquist was certain the nukes would be used again.

"He decided he would survive nuclear war when it came. He created the concept, the design, the specialized equipment to build a self-contained buried world, a sealed biosphere—and called it Eden.

"He wanted to decide who would live in the survival city. After the war, which he knew would come, after the nuclear destruction was unleashed by the irrational minds of mankind, he wanted to start fresh, with nothing but brilliant men and women. He wanted a new world, with himself in charge.

"But Renquist didn't live to take advantage of his creation—he was killed, most likely, in the vaporization of Austin, Texas, just two days before he was to join the people he selected in Eden. The city was sealed off. Its location was always a closely guarded secret, and if someone did survive to try to find it, they could hardly do so—a half mile of rock was avalanched over the site by special machinery automated in advance for that task.

"My great-grandfather Ralf Danik was one of the original groups chosen to survive the war in the radiation-free city. He was an engineer of the waterworks of Eden. My ancestor, and the others with him, had no idea if the system they had created would work. If not, they would all suffocate, or starve, or die of disease. But it did work. And since it had been sealed off before the fallout from the bombed cities came, it was radiation free. The only radiation-free place in the world.

"The people of Eden have never had news of the outside world—none at all. Most of us in Eden believe we are the only people in the world. We live from generation to generation inside the cave. Safe. Secure. But gradually growing weaker. No one knows just why. Perhaps mankind just wasn't made too live so long in caves. By my generation—the fifth—nearly all of us were sterile. And a movement arose.

"Some of us—I was the leader in the effort—said we must dig our way out, that we must attempt to live on the surface again. Preliminary probes with detection equipment were burrowed up in pipes to the surface. They showed higher radiation than normal, less oxygen. But it was liveable, basically. I wanted the tunnel to be widened—I wanted us out.

"That's when the election was held. We had democratic elections of our council every seven years. I ran against a man named Stafford, a scientist who was convinced we should stay underground, that we should devote all our efforts to restore our genetic structure, so that we could have children better adapted to living underground. He was—and is—convinced there is no way for us to exist on the surface. He said our babies could be born in artificial uteruses, if women couldn't give birth.

"My party, the Surface party, won the election handily, but Stafford broke into the century-old storehouses of weapons, and his followers armed themselves and pulled a coup d'état.

21

"I and the others who had been freely elected were hunted down and killed one by one. Our only hope was to reach the surface. And six of us made it—through a series of ancient construction tunnels that had failed to collapse entirely after the burial of the city.

"It was a wild world we encountered. Supplyless, we decided to head north, toward the United States—or where the United States used to be. We were Americans. We hoped to find other Americans. But all we found was death.

"You must understand—underground we had no idea it was winter. Bitter cold. It was never any season underground. We had forgotten the word. We had forgotten the meaning even for bird and cloud—and for one other concept I learned on the perilous trek to this place: *beauty*. For this world of yours, regardless of the dangers, is beautiful. None of us were sorry to leave Eden. We weren't really alive down there.

"I really didn't know exactly where we were heading . . . Our records showed a place called Denver was near the mountains called the Rockies. We found an old map in an abandoned house and some clothing. Rags, but they were warmer than our thin clothing.

"We tried to hunt, with sharpened sticks, but were seldom successful. We ate the few small animals we killed raw, not even having a means of lighting fires until we found a magnifying glass to focus the sun on twigs. Of the six who started out from Eden—myself, Run Dutil, Sysin File, the others—I alone survived to reach this area. And then I was dying, too. I was delirious, out of my senses. And, unknown to me, I was about to be eaten by some huge creature—which your patrol men shot dead. They brought me here, gave me medical attention, and fed me and gave me that delicious thing—coffee—yes, that's it. *Coffee.* Wonderful.

"I used your rapid-learning tapes, listened to them while I slept. Absolutely an amazing achievement. Sleep learning. Fantastic. Your kind Dr. Schecter told me to rest after I had eaten, and attached the sleep-learning device. It told me all about your fabulous city. Century City is full of art, of fresh air, and—love. Yes, love. Something we had forgotten. We though of procreation only as a process, not as the result of the love between male and female. I have learned so much of your people already. Eden will only live if it becomes one of your allied free cities. Open to the world. Dedicated to the fighting of the Soviet occupiers. Help me, Rockson—come back with me and help me free Eden."

"Wow," Rockson said. He didn't know what else to say.

"You must go to Eden with Peth Danik, Rockson," Rath said. "Not only for their sake, but for our sake. To stop Stafford, the mad dictator of Eden, from releasing Factor Q."

"*Factor Q?* What's that, Danik?"

"Rockson, I am sorry to say that when Stafford raided the ancient war supplies stored in Eden, he found a terrible weapon—a germ-warfare canister. Factor Q. It's sort of a virus really—that spreads on the wind. Once released on the surface—which is what Stafford has threatened to do—no human will be alive within a week. The canister must be incinerated without being opened. Burned totally at high

23

temperature. That means of its deactivation must be accomplished before Stafford uses it. Stafford says if the people protest his rule, if they wish to try to live on the surface despite his warnings, he will release the virus above Eden. So that no one could ever hope to live on the surface."

"I see," Rock said grimly.

"Stafford's a real Jim Jones case," Rath added. "Stafford must be stopped. Will you try, Rockson?"

Rockson sighed. "We're snowbound . . ."

"You made it up to Alaska and back once in the winter."

"With sled dogs, and an Eskimo guide. I don't have either here . . . Danik, if I mounted an expedition, say a six- or seven-man attack force, can you lead me to Eden?"

"I don't know the way there. I just wandered here. I don't know the location of Eden. God, I'm sorry, Rockson." Danik buried his thin face in his hands.

"You have to find a way to Eden, Rockson," Rath demanded. "You *will* find a way. You're the Doomsday Warrior."

"Thanks for your confidence. But there are things I can't do—like miracles."

"You'll find a way."

# Chapter 3

Danik lay down in his warm feather bed and looked up at the softly glowing ceiling above him. "Century City," he said softly to himself. "I am in Century City, a free American city. There is life, life vibrant and healthy, out here in the wilderness of America. Here are people, not sickly diseased mutations, not cannibals as Stafford had claimed—but good, brave Americans."

Danik reached over to the table and took up the sleep-learning earphones and placed them on his head. He closed his eyes. Dr. Schecter had told him to relax, to rest and listen to this particular tape: "Accounts of the Exploits of Ted Rockson, by Detroit Green." Schecter reasoned that on hearing of the exploits of Ted Rockson, Danik's unconscious would have to admit the possibility that Ted Rockson *could* do the impossible. Namely, that Rockson could go to

Eden with his small squad, defeat Stafford, prevent Factor Q from being unleashed. Schecter believed, along with the psychiatric staff, that Danik's blocked memories of his trek might be released *if* Danik believed there was *hope*. "You'll remember enough of your trek to lead our man to Eden," Schecter had encouraged. "You *will*."

Danik sighed. He put on the earphones and lay back trying to relax. He did want to hear of Rockson's exploits. Danik wanted to know more about this man with the white streak in his hair and mismatched eyes. The man they called the Doomsday Warrior.

Everyone was depending on him to remember. And he couldn't. The only thing he remembered of the trek was coming out of the half-collapsed tunnel from Eden with his companions in the nighttime. And following the star—the North Star. Then all was a blank until the moment he was being carried by two men into Century City. They'd carried him up to a sheer mountain wall, banged on the rocks as if they were knocking on a door. Then, amazingly, a doorway *had* opened and they had moved on into a long green-lit corridor, the doorway sealing behind them silently. He remembered other people—men and gorgeous tall healthy women—coming to meet the men who carried him. These people wore white uniforms.

He had been placed on the table and wheeled down a maze of corridors to a white room. He remembered tubes being stuck into his arms and a kindly old man the others called Dr. Schecter leaning over him and doing things with instruments that beeped and clicked. Then there had been the blissful warm darkness. And when he awoke—the doctor had said,

"How are you?"

The man called Rath had come, questioned him briefly, and told him to rest again. In response to Danik's own questions they had given him his first sleep-learning tape, the one that told the history of Century City. He could practically recite it:

On one fateful fall day in 1989, the skies over America had filled with death. Death coming in the form of a thousand nuke warheads fired by the Soviet Union, a surprise attack that was to devastate the United States. A surprise attack that would raise clouds of deadly fallout that would also make much of the world—including the Soviet Union—a radioactive desert. Madness. And yet it happened . . . But that was only the beginning, not the end.

Oh, what a story came next. The building of Century City. The story of a proud and brave people—Americans, surviving. Men and women trapped in their vehicles in the miles-long highway tunnel near Denver, sealed off from the fallout by avalanches, had dug out. They'd seen what had happened and sealed themselves in again. There were trailer trucks of supplies on that buried road, and men and women with all sorts of skills. They endured. They had slowly, over a hundred years, carved out this fantastic city, and still fought the Soviet occupiers of America. Century City, the product of the survivors of a nation of tinkerers—tinkerers like Edison, Ford, Du Mont, tinkerers with visions, with no holds on their imagination—because they were *free*.

The tape had told Danik of the century-plus of struggle against the brutal occupiers, and of the millions of less fortunate Americans that lived in fortress cities of the conquering armies of Russia, as

27

slaves—slaves that toiled for their masters sixteen hours a day seven days a week, to supply the Reds with all their clothing, weapons, and foodstuffs.

But there was more, much more to America than slavery. Danik had learned that a league of hidden free cities—some small military bases, some large complexes like Century City, existed in the Rocky Mountains. These hidden bases were waging a successful guerrilla war against the Russians. And the leader of that epic struggle was the man he had met just that afternoon, the man they called the Doomsday Warrior. Which was why Danik was anxious to listen to Rockson's exploits now. He adjusted the earphones; Danik fell asleep and dreamed. The dream he dreamed—compliments of the sleep tape—told the story of the Doomsday Warrior. From the time Ted Rockson had wandered into Century City as a teenage boy: Rockson's parents, who had lived with him far into the wilderness, were killed by a KGB patrol. Rockson had journeyed through the wilderness to Century City virtually unarmed. He ate what he found or killed. The distance was a thousand miles. Once in the free fortress-city, he quickly rose through the ranks of Freefighters to command position, first as a lieutenant, eventually becoming a general, and then, finally commander of all the Resistance forces.

The tape summarized, in varying detail, many of Rockson's exploits, especially the last. It had been a mission to the Arctic Circle itself, after a madman named Killov, who threatened the world from the bitter darkness of the northern winter with deadly atomic missiles. Ted Rockson had trekked to the north and challenged Killov and his KGB army with a mere handful of companions — *the Rock Team*, as he called them

The Rock Team were seven individuals of rare skills and fighting abilities: Besides Rockson, it consisted of

*Detroit Green*, the bullnecked black man — a crack shot and a fearsome opponent in hand-to-hand. Green was a champion grenade thrower. He always carried twin bandoliers with dozens of his "pineapples" attached to them across his chest.

Then there was *Chen*, the martial arts expert with the pencil-thin moustache. He had taught Rockson his fighting skills. Chen carried a beltload of *shuriken*, or star-knives. Some of the five- and six-pointed metal stars were for slicing throats at a hundred yards. Others were *more* lethal, carrying mini plastic charges of explosive, for ripping apart enemy units.

*McCaughlin*, a seven-foot-tall bear of a man, not light on his feet of course, but a real powerhouse, was a human battering ram most useful when a door that couldn't be opened had to be. The crew-cut Scots-American was a crack shot with the 9mm Liberator rifle. But more important, he was a real humorist. Often, he was the morale builder of the Rock Team. When things got rough, when all hope appeared lost, McCaughlin's gentle wit and wry jokes saved the day. He was a must on every mission.

Then there was *Archer*, the near-mute mountain man who Rockson had once saved from a quicksand pool. Archer was the oddest of the bunch. He lived deep in the twisting maze of conduit tunnels deep below Century City, preferring isolation and quiet to companionship. And why not? Archer, named thus because of his fantastic homemade metal crossbow and the special arrows that he always carried, had lived alone most of his life. Until he was found in his desperate condition by Rockson. Now Archer had allegiance to Rockson and Rockson alone. Because he always wore his same bearskin clothing, and seldom if ever bathed, some inhabitants of the rather neat underground city shunned him — and he shunned them. Still, when out in the open, his scent wasn't too bad, and he was a good man to have around.

*Scheransky* was the latest addition to the team led by the Doomsday Warrior. He was a Russian defector, who liked to describe himself as "Russian, not Soviet." He was proud of his people and their ingenuity and many achievements, and lived for the day when the hated dictatorship of his native land could be brought down to let democracy finally reign. A short man, he had once been chubby, but now this dark-eyed, blond-haired technical wizard had slimmed down, gotten hard and muscled in the fight for freedom.

*Rona Wallender*, the only female member of the Rockson team, had been left behind on the Rock Team mission to Alaska. Not that the Amazon-like tanned beauty had wanted to be left behind. She was a crack shot, and trained in survival and the martial arts. Frequently, Rona was Rockson's companion when he hunted bear and deer in the wilderness of the Rockies. And the stunning redhead, all five foot ten of her, never failed to bag her share of dangerous quarry. She had been Rockson's lover for years. Not that the Doomsday Warrior didn't dally here and there with other females from time to time.

Danik learned that last Rock Team mission to save freedom had ended with a triumph for his forces of liberty. While the Rock Team had engaged Killov's army in a deadly firefight in the Arctic darkness, the Doomsday Warrior had commandeered a Soviet jet and chased after the deadly missile launched by KGB head Killov. Rockson had destroyed Killov's deadly missile in midair. Then Rockson had crash-landed in the desert. And after being captured by a Soviet patrol, he had encountered a strange megastorm. The nature of that storm, and its consequences for Rockson, was classified material, and not available on tape.

The taped account of the adventure finished with the Doomsday Warrior staggering into Century City's south portal nine months ago, about as near death as Danik had been.

When he awoke, Danik had only one thing in mind. To travel to Eden with this man-among-men, with this hero of the twenty-first century, Ted Rockson, and his team of Freefighters. If Danik should die, then it would be a noble death, to be among such brave warriors.

After a breakfast of fresh scrambled hawk eggs and coffee, served in his room by a pretty orderly named Janet, Danik eagerly set off down the corridors he was becoming familiar with to his morning meeting with the entire Rock Team. Danik was elated. He *had* remembered something. Not much, but something. Perhaps it would be enough.

# Chapter 4

Rockson had gathered most of the Rock Team in the Security office. They sat with notepads in front of them, around the shiny-surfaced conference table. Rath was there of course too. The door opened a moment after the combat veterans had all arrived. Rock looked up, expecting to see Danik. But instead it was Rona. All dressed up in full combat gear.

"Rona, what the hell are you doing down here?" he bellowed.

"I want in on this one, Rock. You left me out of the Alaska mission—I'm going on this one."

"Like hell you are. I'm only taking members of my northern team. The winter team. You're out."

"I'm in."

Rock sighed, "Look Rona, there probably isn't a mission at all. I assume you're familiar by now with the events of the past few days; our visitor from Eden?"

She nodded.

"Well, Danik doesn't remember enough to lead us *anywhere*. And even if he did, unless we figure out some way to get through a thousand miles of waist-high snow and subzero temperatures—even these

33

men, all veterans of the Alaska mission—won't be able to do a thing."

Before the argument died down, Danik came in on schedule and seated himself. After introductions, Danik told of his new recollections. They were sketchy. Danik couldn't trace his course on the map Rockson had spread on the table. There was no need for such maps in Eden. He *did* remember some landmarks along the route he had taken from Eden. The team eagerly listened to these recollections.

"I remember we crossed a river—a shallow thing that my friend Run Dutil said was the Rio Grande. Then the next thing I recall, two days later, are some odd-shaped rocks—about fifty feet high. Carved by the surface winds, I suppose. One looked like a whale—I've seen your pictures of whales."

"Does that formation ring any bells?" Rock asked.

No one was familiar with it.

"Anything else?" the Doomsday Warrior asked.

Danik offered him some scattered bizarre landmarks, descriptions of the places he and his friends had taken shelter on their trek:

A five-story-tall teepee-shaped souvenir store and restaurant, abandoned no doubt in the first few days after the 1989 war. There, two of his friends, Sysin Print and File Format, had died, he didn't know of what. Perhaps of a combination of the cold and lack of food.

Scheransky asked, "What is the derivation of your friends' names? It sounds like computer talk."

"Most of us in Eden, those that don't have a famous family name, are named by computer at our first birthday. The names are the result of a registrar

34

picking the keys of the birth registry computer at random, until a systems message is printed. That becomes the child's name."

"Please go on," Rath said, *"and no more interruptions."*

Danik related that the rest of the desperate party of Edenites had gone on, hopefully straight north, and reached an immense, beautifully arched, perfectly preserved stone bridge going nowhere, sitting in a shallow desert lake. There, two more friends of Danik's company had expired as they all huddled together for warmth in an old concrete-slab pile. The dead were entombed behind a loose foundation stone in the bridge. The temperature had dropped from that day onward. On the last leg of the journey to Colorado, Danik and his last surviving companion, Run Dutil, had tried to make notes and measurements of their course, using a toy compass Run Dutil had found in a collapsed building near the strange stone bridge.

The snows kept falling, and they found shelter. Dutil had died in a strange building filled with plastic statues of Presidents of the United States.

"That's all I can recollect," Danik ended, "If I had only taken that notebook of Dutil's out of his dead frozen hand—but I didn't. I didn't even bury him, I— I left him sitting there. I was . . . so *weak*. I can't give you a clue as to where that strange building with plastic Presidents is."

At the mention of the last odd sight, Rona shouted out, "I think I know the place he means—it's the Presidential Museum outside of Colorado Springs. Once, years ago, when I was a teenager, I went there with a scouting team. We were looking for signs of a new Soviet-made road—and found it too—blew it to hell. But anyway, we came across this old building half collapsed. We went inside and there was a plastic JFK in his rocker, and a glass case containing plastic statues of the three men who made the first Moon trip—Armstrong, Aldrin, and Conrad."

"That's it," Danik said, elated. "You're right. There were those astronaut statues too."

"Great," exclaimed Rath, "So, Rockson, we can get your attack team to Colorado Springs—a mere two days' journey. Then the notebook can steer you on the rest of the way."

Rockson was only somewhat encouraged. "*If* the notebook is still there, and *if* Dutil's scribblings—he didn't have any training in direction finding—make sense. Two big ifs, Rath."

Rona reached across the table to touch the cold thin hands of the stranger. She smiled warmly, asked, "Mr. Dutil, is there anything else, anything at all?"

Dutil spewed out a few other descriptions of the trek—just terrain descriptions. Crumbling cliffs, a twisting canyon of sandstone.

Rock couldn't hazard a guess at Danik's route. Unless Danik remembered where he'd started out from, as a reference point, they hadn't much to go on. And if he knew that, they'd be busying themselves to get there.

"I agree; we go to the President's museum and then look for the notebook," Rock said. "We'll at least give Run Dutil a decent burial, if the animals haven't had him by now. If the notebook has anything useful in it we can proceed from there. But I need some ideas for

36

travel in this damned weather."

"I know a way for us to get to the President museum, and to get all the way to Eden, despite the snow," Rona stated firmly.

"How?"

"Uh uh. First you promise to take me if I have a way for us to get there, *then* I tell you. Agreed?"

Rockson wanted to know her idea. He said, "Agreed."

Rona told him "Dogs. We make sleds and use dogs just like you did in Alaska."

"Rona, there are no dogs here in Century City."

"Yes, there are. You remember those snow-wolf pups that were a gift of the New Omicron City Council upon your safe return from the Alaskan mission?"

"Yeah — some gift. They near took one of my fingers off — you can still see the stitches. I sent them down to the kennel area for study. Haven't heard a thing —"

"They're all grown up, and since they never lived in the wild, they're mellowed. They're positively almost like dogs. Still a bit wild — they have three rows of teeth — but I think they might do handily to pull sleds. They have lot of spirit, anyway. Maybe . . ."

"Hmmm. Maybe won't do — besides, they would be only one year old now."

Rona was undaunted. "I went to see them this morning. They're really big, Rock. You should see them. Kathleen down in Breeding said they're training well; they heel and sit and give you their paw and everything. And there's only been a few — well, accidents . . ."

37

"Accidents?"

"Well, they nipped a few of Conyer's fingers off. But that's because he had the smell of some meat he was feeding them earlier on his fingers."

"Great. *Forget it, Rona.* Any other ideas on how to beat the snow?"

"How about getting some skis and skiing to Mexico?" McCaughlin suggested. "Course, I don't ski so well. It was okay to have skis on when hanging on to a dog sled, but I don't think I personally could manage such a trek on skis."

Detroit said they could never ski a thousand-plus miles either. Archer shrugged. He took off his floppy hat, because it was warm in the room. Danik, who had never seen Archer's remodeled forehead, gasped.

McCaughlin smiled. "Don't be alarmed, Danik. Archer had some crystals implanted up there in his head. On our mission north last year, some hairy things smashed an ax down on his skull and did some damage. We took Archer to an advanced Eskimo hospital, and they patched him up real funny. The crystals that fill that gap in his skull look pretty, and they spark blue and red whenever Archer tries to think too profound—ain't that right, partner?"

Archer sort of growled something, and his beard of tangled black moved up and down like he was a chewing something he didn't like. He put his hat back on.

"Any other ideas on how to trek in this bad weather?" Rock asked, getting the show back on the road.

There were none, except snowshoe trekking. And that would take longer than walking. Time was the crucial factor.

Rock sighed. "Let's have a look at these dogs, Rona. Lead on."

The rest of the Freefighter team went over maps trying to find the landmarks Danik had reported seeing on the way north. Rock and Rona rode the elevator down to X level and entered the animal-breeding area. The smell of cow dung and hay and so on made Rona sneeze. But Rock inhaled deeply. "Ah, just a country boy at heart."

"Give me a break," Rona said. "I get hay fever."

Breeding Section was cavernous carved-out area about 100 meters by 90 meters, with a high arched ceiling that sported hundreds of full-spectrum lights. It felt sort of like sunlight on the skin. The *baaing* of sheep and the *mooing* of cows from the many rough-hewn wooden stalls attested to the success of the efforts of Dr. Kathleen McCullough and her staff.

McCullough, wearing a white lab smock over her rather tubby middle-aged body was carrying a clip-board, met them halfway up to the canine area. "Hi," she smiled, revealing several gold fillings. "I was told you would be interested in seeing our wolf-dogs, Rock."

"Rona no doubt told you that. I'm sceptical. But lead on."

They went past a stall containing several cows nibbling on bales of hay. "Sweet, aren't they? They're a black-and-white milk cow called the Guernsey—or the rad-resistant twenty-first century equivalent anyway. They give lots of milk. We supply all the city's milk and much of Century City's meat from right here—and that's not all. In Z Sector, we're now doing important back-breeding of many rad-altered species too. Schecter had done some unique gene-splicing research that enabled the staff to begin restoring much of the vanished species of the Rockies to their original look—without altering their inherited resistance to the radiation levels hereabouts."

"It's comforting to see," Rock noted as they passed the fox cages, "that these red fox no longer have multiple razor-horns with venom inside them. Almost got killed by one of their wild relatives once."

"Someday these back-bred species will be put on the surface to breed and multiply in the wild, but right now there are precious few of them. And we have to toughen this species up. Or make them craftier. Otherwise their relatives—the horned variety—will make mincemeat out of them."

Kathleen McCullough was an affable type, and Rockson wanted to linger and admire the handiwork of her section, but they had to rush onward to the kennels. "I'll demand a longer tour some other time, Kathleen."

"Come any time."

They entered the K-9 area. The barking was intense and immediate when the door was opened. And not only barking—some sort of God-awful high-pitched howls, several of them.

"Is that the—"

"Yes, the snow-wolf pups have become noisy in their old age."

"Jeez," Rock said. "I don't know if I could take a lot of those horrible howls."

Rona laughed. "They are really not so bad once they stop howling."

40

They went to a grillwork window, and as Rockson leaned close to the glass, slavering snarling triple-row-of-teeth mouths slammed against the metal grating.

Rock leaped back. "God, I didn't expect that."

"You have to be introduced to these wolf-dogs by someone they like — or else. This one," said Kathleen, opening the next door as Rockson flattened himself against the wall and put his hand on the butt of his shotpistol, "is the biggest one — one hundred and ten pounds of fury. We call her Class Act, because she has such a beautiful silvery coat of fur. Come on in, and meet her."

Kathleen approached the giant furry wolf-dog and petted its head. "Hi, it's me — we're going to come in now — we have some dog yummies for you and some visitors — please be nice now — no biting?"

A snarl in response. Kathleen said, "Now, be a nice girl."

"Scaredy cat — you can hide behind me," Rona said.

"I'm not *afraid*, just *cautious*," Rockson retorted, and petted the head of the brute. The wolf-dog's fur was cool and fluffy. She went to lick his hand. "She's a bit bigger than I expected," Rock said, "but she's nice."

The triple row of teeth could be seen easily, as the dog yawned and sat down on its huge haunches. It seemed to be smiling.

"Good dog," Kathleen said, petting it once or twice more.

"Rock, I think she likes you."

"Yeah," Rockson said ambivalently. "Are the males bigger?" He petted the thing's head again. The dog

41

responded by rubbing up against his leg, a move that almost tumbled him over. "Man, this dog has some strength."

"And so do her brothers and sisters. Yes, the males are a bit bigger—but less intelligent." Kathleen winked at Rona, and Rona laughed.

Rona, recovering, said, "They're certainly strong enough to pull a few of our itty-bitty sleds to Mexico."

# Chapter 5

Rockson reconvened the attack team, and told them it might be possible after all to use sleds and these strange dogs.

Danik was eager to go right away, but Rockson told him that several days at a minimum would be needed to prepare. "Get some sleep, take a whole lot of vitamins, build yourself up, Danik. We can't go slow. It will be an arduous trip—assuming we find the notebook and it helps us find our way to Eden."

While Danik was recuperating, the dogs were rounded up; and training them on a crash basis was begun. The extensive experience the Rock Team had gotten handling sled dogs in the Alaska mission* proved invaluable.

To speed things up, Rockson assigned teams to handle specific tasks. Detroit and McCaughlin were in charge of production of the super-lightweight plastic sleds, handicrafting the nylon lead ropes, and selecting some skis.

Rockson and Chen rounded up maps of every area

*See Doomsday Warrior #9.

between the city and mid-Mexico. Rockson also compiled a set of history tapes and slides of a thousand sites south of Colorado. This was for Danik's viewing. He sent them to his room. But Danik sent back word that he couldn't remember the route he'd taken north except by the strange ruined twentieth-century tourist attractions he had already told them about.

Of course weapons were a must; Rockson and Chen went through C.C.'s extensive armory, selecting the lightest, deadliest of the lot. Rock picked up two compound bows with two-hundred-pound pulls, and Chen loaded up on exploding star-knives. They would take along the usual standard Freefighter equipment too—a set of Liberator 9mm rifles and x-pattern shot-pistols.

They needed a complete roster of foodstuffs and sundry supplies from the quartermaster. These supplies included inertial navigation compasses with illuminated faces, sextants, pemmican—the highly condensed high-calorie food for trekking in cold weather—McCaughlin's special biscuits (just add snow and cook), salt, tea and coffee, egg powder, and bacon. Plus some jam, a few loafs of pumpernickel bread, assorted pots and pans. They would also bring sleeping bags, Coleman lamps, a Primus stove and fuel for it—though it could burn animal fat. They intended to hunt on the way south. They'd need warm blankets, an emergency first-aid kit, and a dozen other items. Century City was a storehouse of such items and there was no problem assembling the roster.

Rona and Archer—sort of beauty and the beast— were in charge of actually getting the dogs trained and attached to the sleds in time for a test run through the town square in three days. Everyone moved efficiently.

Rockson, four days after they had a destination, proudly announced to Security Chief Rath that they were ready to go. Danik was up and around, and he came into Rath's office just as Rockson was reporting.

"If all goes well," Rock said to the strange visitor, "we will get you to Eden—despite the harsh winter conditions."

"Rockson," Danik said, "I understand you are going to use sleds pulled by ferocious mutated wolves. Isn't that—rather unusual? Why not use snowmobiles? I understand there are several here in—"

"Equipment breaks down," Rockson explained, "One cog busts and you have a useless hunk of metal. Believe me, nothing has yet replaced the reliability of dogs for long hauls over snow. *These* particular wolf-dogs are strong. If they can be controlled, and I think they can be, they will be more than satisfactory for the job. They can eat what we kill for them on the way also. We would need a few filling stations for a bunch of snowmobiles."

"I see," said Danik. "Yes, of course."

Rath had been working too. He had contacted a small Indian settlement in Arizona by subspace communication. The settlement, Yumak City, would have some horses, he said, for the final leg of the journey to Eden, if they couldn't divert to that place. "I don't suppose you hope to use sleds in Mexico. The snow is very light down there, though it's six feet deep around these parts."

"I was counting on you to arrange such a thing," Rockson said. "Schecter told me you were working on it. Who do I see down there in Yumak?"

"Ask for Chief Smokestone."

45

# Chapter 6

At the first light of dawn, the eighth day after Danik had wandered into Century City's domain, they were ready. The Rock Team was in the main exit tunnel on the south face of Carson Mountain about to set out. Under the greenish lights of the wide concrete waiting area, Rockson inspected the team of six ferocious wolf-dogs squirming in front of his sled. He hoped they wouldn't all of a sudden decide they wanted human meat rather than some of the dried bear meat they were bringing along for them. He turned to see the two other sleds lined up behind him. The howling of the damned half-wild animals they were depending on for locomotion was abominable. He hoped the giant steel door would track open soon. The echo of the howling was unbearable.

If the dogs worked out, he was confident they could go a thousand miles. They had all the weapons and equipment he had wanted — and more.

There was always certain standard equipment on any trek — the shotpistols, the power batons, the

Liberator rifles. But each Freefighter had his own set of special weapons of his own choice.

Rockson carried a versatile balisong knife in his belt, plus an exploding baton. He also had, on his sled, an aluminum power-bow and a good-sized quiver of killing arrows. It was a bow similar to Rona's but with even more pull. For silencing guards, should they reach Eden and take on such opponents as would be there, he brought along a set of Greek garroting chains.

Archer was of course well armed—he even slept with his special homemade steel crossbow cradled in his arms. Rock knew he carried a grab bag of good weapons under those multiple smelly bearskins he wore. The bearded mountain man had, for one thing, lengths of rope and steel cable. He liked to combine his arrows and these cords for grappling purposes—or just to lasso some unfortunate enemy. Over his shoulder on a ratty leather strap, he wore a knapsack full of ancient musket weapons all loaded with grapeshot and nails.

Chen of course carried sixteen explosive and forty nonexplosive shuriken. He also carried a yarawa stick—for jabbing pressure points—and a set of nunchaku.

Detroit Green carried twin bandoliers of grenades strapped across his brawny chest. Also, a set of throwing blades. Plus an ancient western Colt .45 Rock had given him on his birthday.

McCaughlin was the one with the power-brass knuckles. It added to the force of his fists; the explosive-bolt knuckles would do what the crushing power of his massive shoulders wouldn't do to a door or wall or person. The big trail cook also had taken to carrying a boomerang—he had been taught its use by a friendly Australian comrade some time ago.*

Rona carried her crossbow of aluminum and a quiver of arrows. Lighter than Archer's heavy homemade weapon of steel and wood, yet deadly. Rona Wallender's arrows were tipped with poisons. Lots of different poisons. Plus she carried her "lady's weapon"—a tiny derringer-type pistol with .22 bullets in a handle clip. Bullets tipped with poison too.

Scheransky carried the Russian weapons of choice—the bludgeon, plus a Dragunov sniper rifle and the laser-honed short sword in his belt.

Thus armed, the Freefighters could take on platoons of Soviet special forces. And they might have to, Rockson thought. They might just have to do just that . . . For America was crawling with the Soviet invaders.

"Too bad we can't take along a tank," McCaughlin joked as the loaded sleds and their earnest drivers waited for the steel doors to open to the outside world of terror.

"Yeah," Rockson quipped, "or a few pieces of artillery. Snow or no snow, I doubt the Soviets have stopped patrolling the area between here and Mexico. They *like* winter, right, Scheransky?"

"Indubitably, Russians like winter. Why, in Moscow, we even eat ice cream in weather like this . . . " Scheransky said.

"Make mine tutti-frutti," said Detroit. "Look, the sun is out."

*See Doomsday Warrior #7.

It *was* out. The door slid open to reveal a clear day. There was a pleasant pink-ocher sunrise sending multiple beams of light up over the craggy ice-laden peaks of the Rocky Mountains to the east.

"Red sky in morning, sailor take warning . . . " Rockson muttered.

"What did you say?" Detroit yelled over the din of the eager wolf-dogs.

"The weather could change for the worse soon," Rock rephrased.

Archer slid his sled right past the Doomsday Warrior's the minute the three teams of six dogs each had gotten out on the slope heading down from Carson Mountain. The damned dogs obeyed his every mutter. Perhaps it was his smell that ingratiated the big mountainman to the dogs, Rock thought. Whatever it was, Archer was the only one who didn't have to use a whip on the beasts to steer them.

Those Freefighters who weren't driving the sleds rode alongside, tethered by rope, sliding along on their short steel skis. Danik was apparently having a ball on his skis, despite very little training in their use. He slid up alongside Rockson and said, "The sunrise is so beautiful. So many colors. It's sad my friends are not here to see us and this beautiful day."

"Just a typical sunrise," Rock smiled, "Evidently you like the surface world."

"Yes, it is most fascinating and beautiful."

For hours they traversed country Rock knew well. The landscape was muted by gentle deep waves of brilliant white. The snow goggles — slits in plastic — helped shield their eyes. Still, Rockson was relieved when some clouds showed up to dim the scenery a bit.

"Mush, you mutated Americansky huskies, *mush*," Scheransky cried out. It was his turn to navigate the first sled and he was doing it with relish. Rona steered the second sled expertly alongside him. Rock trailed, happy to give up the lead. The wolf-dogs howled their triple-tooth best and pulled the sleds mightily. At first they were difficult to control, but then the "dogs" settled down. They pulled the heavily laden sleds like they were lightweight paper.

"I think this is going to work fine," Rock yelled over the snorting and howling to Rona, "if they stop making so much noise."

"They'll quiet down—they're excited and happy to be out in the real world, that's all."

With cracks of the whips, they were speeding along at fifty miles per hour, sliding down the steep incline of a blanket of hard packed snow. *The best way to travel*, Rock thought.

Rockson considered the plan rather loosely conceived. Lots of things never done before were being attempted here. He hoped to god it would all work. The sleds, for instance. Would they hold up? Sure, they'd last for the trek to the damned President museum or whatever the hell it was. But if they went further—would they hold up? And Danik—he was doing fine so far, but he was a delicate sort. Might not fare well in hardships to come. And the mission would have to be aborted if the notebook they were after was missing. Or if the notes in it didn't have useful bearings. And things were even vaguer for when—and if—they got to Eden. Danik wanted them to hide in the lake area of the underground biosphere and wait for members of his dissenter group to join them, and *then* make plans in concert with these Edenites. Rock didn't like this plan. He would think of another one, if and when they got there.

He half-laughed. Only the fate of the world hung on these many variables. God, what if Stafford had already decided to release the deadly vial of germs into the atmosphere? Nobody knew what fiendish concoction Factor Q was, or how to immunize anyone against it. The one thing Danik did know about the deadly virus was that it took only one day to kill after a person was infected. Great. Rock watched the parka-clad woman slide along on skis.

Rona had earned her entry into the mission. Without her initiatives, it would never have been possible. She was some lady. And Rock looked forward to sharing his sleeping bag with the leggy redhead. A bonus for having her along. The guys would understand — wouldn't they? Of course, McCaughlin would tease — but what the hell. And *Scheransky* — Rock was proud of the man.

The Russian was an asset. A man who Rock had come to admire, as much for his courage and openmindedness as for his technical knowledge. Rockson couldn't get over the change in Scheransky. The Russian defector was quite different from when Rock had first met him, right after he'd parachuted down from a Soviet plane. Then, Scheransky had been a pudgy techie, brainwashed into believing most if not all of the Communist party line. Now he was lean and hard, a seasoned veteran of the Freefighter forces. His allegiance was to freedom now, freedom and strength. The rest of the team were friends and worthy members of the human race. Rock worried that some of them might not survive the whole journey. Just a hunch. *Who?*

It was near dark when Rockson decided, by taking sightings with his navigation equipment, that they were nearing the Hall of President's museum. The Freefighters had shuffled positions again. Now, Detroit and Chen were hanging onto the sled that the Russian drove. Each wore the short metal skis that had special almost-frictionless bottoms under their boots. That lessened the weight the dogs had to pull.

Rockson's sled followed. He drove its six fan-hitched wolf-huskies relentlessly, and they never tired. McCaughlin and Archer were sliding along holding on each to their own handle behind him.

Rock hoped that at the end of each day's trek they could find some sort of shelter—a rock overhang, anything. They had a survival tent, but there was a suspicious wind rising from the east. The worst storms came out of the Great Plains, where they could build and build, unencumbered by mountains. He feared the worst.

# Chapter 7

Rock watched the towering black clouds building over the hills. Though it wasn't snowing, the increasing winds coming from the blackness ahead whipped through his down coat and threatened to tear off his fur-flapped hat.

Most snow clouds are gray. Black snowclouds could mean acid snow — the conical-flaked *death* snows. No one could predict when the black snow would come to devastate an area; they just came out of nowhere.

A biting cold hit just as the sky became totally dark. It was as if the sun had set, and yet it was an hour before sunset.

Rockson, anxious to make their goal before all hell broke loose, pushed their teams to the utmost. The cold ate into his hands, his arms, his legs, despite the thermal layers of synseal and goose down. The others too by their grim expressions were feeling the sixty-below temperature — and realizing the danger.

There was only open, rolling terrain ahead, but hopefully they could reach the cliffs he could see miles ahead, find shelter before the storm hit. Worry about finding the museum later.

Within minutes, as the seven brave Freefighters whipped their half-wild teams to a frenzied pace, the storm overtook them. A thunderous howl of wind-blown snow obscured the way, and in that blown white snow appeared black specks — the dreaded black snow.

"Faster, we've got to go faster. Shine your flashlights ahead; use your compasses. Keep going west-south-west. We've got to find shelter."

The sled he was riding started to shimmy in the wind; the dogs were howling, their voices an eerie cross between wolf howl and dogs' growl. Lightning and thunder rent the air. The black specks increased. Rockson got the first hit on his lips. It burned. Acid snow, all right.

There appeared a dozen, then a hundred, smoking tiny holes in his snow suit. The acid flakes were eating into his clothing.

He pulled the hood down over his face — he couldn't see ahead anyway, so he just kept the luminous compass in sight through the tiny hole he left to see through. "Faster, faster," he yelled, whipping the howlers.

It was totally dark now; they were plunging ahead at breakneck speed, but they had no choice. The super-strong wolf-dogs were the one thing in their favor. Snow-wolf pelts were special — they were immune to acid snows, the result of a hundred years of genetic mutation after the nuke war. The dogs would keep going. But the acid snow, though it didn't blind the teams, still stung their eyes. Therefore the howls of pain. The dogs wanted to stop and huddle together, protecting their eyes. But if they stopped, the humans they pulled would be burned to skeletons in a matter of ten minutes.

Only the whip kept them going.

Rock had to look ahead — he uncovered his eyes. It hurt, but he had to look. *There*. Through the swirling gray-blackness, Rock dimly saw a shape—the cliffs. "We're almost there, keep behind me, I'm going to find a niche in the rocks for us to hole up in," he shouted, the wind nearly drowning his words.

It didn't take long once they reached the jagged jumbled rocks of the cliffs to find a deep rock overhang. In seconds they were out of the snow and wind. With their flashtorches lit, they unhooded and removed their outer clothing and applied ointment to their stung faces and eyes. Detroit had a space between his left glove and his coat, and the skin was badly burned there. But by some miracle that was the only injury. The parkas weren't impervious to the acid snow, but they had some resistant quality. Schecter had synthesized the material the parkas were made of. Good old Schecter.

There were some small gnarled tree stumps in the rock shelter, "Joshua trees," said Detroit. "Thousands of years old."

Rock carefully unhitched the teams of dogs and tied them to the stumpy trees, then Chen and he applied ointment to the wolf-dogs' big red saucer eyes.

They seemed to sense that they were being treated for their own good, and the salivating teeth-aplenty creatures docilely accepted the ministrations.

That accomplished, Rockson said, "Maybe we can get a fire burning—there're lots of broken branches and some dried grass in clumps here and there." It was a good idea, for the temperature still hovered around sixty below. In no time at all, wood and kindling had been gathered and a roaring fire lit. Rockson sat down close to the fire on the bare earth. Ah, this was better.

He felt something uncomfortable—maybe a root—

under him.

He stood up to see what the offending object was, and picked up what looked like the femur bone of a human skeleton. "Hey, look at this—seems like we're not the only ones to ever stop here . . ."

"Nor the unluckiest. I wonder what he died of," Chen said.

Rona said, "Maybe we'd better have a look around . . ."

One of the bigger of the wolf-dogs, the one that Class Act seemed to always huddle with, began growling. His fierce red eyes, glowing in the campfire light, fixated on Rockson. The beast yowled and lunged forward, snapping his restraint, his salivating triple jaws heading straight for the Doomsday Warrior.

"Drop the bone," Rona said, throwing her weight against Rockson, pushing him aside in the nick of time. Rockson rolled and came to a stand. He had dropped the bone, yet was preparing for another onslaught from the wild dog. But the dog just lost interest and sat down.

Chen put his exploding star-knife down. "I was just about to throw it at the damned animal. We would have been out one damned good dog," he said. "Good thing it quieted down."

"I wonder what upset it?" Rockson mused, carefully going over and retying the creature. It didn't even growl. Then Rock went over to the bone again and started lifting it. Instantly the dog began growling. He dropped it.

"Looks like it isn't you but the bone the dog doesn't like," Rona observed.

"Okay with me," Rockson said. "I'll leave the

damned bone alone." He walked to the fire. "Mc-Caughlin, do you have that dried caribou meat? The dogs might be a bit hungry. Maybe that's what's bugging them."

"I'll get right to it, Rock. I'll fix it up, roast it on a spit over this here fire. And I'll fix us humans up some good grub too."

"Took the words right out of my mouth. Save the fatty parts for our dogs. They deserve some food. They sure are doing their job. Glad I thought to use them for this trek." Rock shot a glance at Rona and winked.

In a matter of twenty minutes, they were all chomping on the delicious dried meat of the caribou. The howling winds were subsiding outside, and they were warm. The snow had become white, and the hissing acid death was being dissolved by pretty white snowflake crystals.

Detroit took some of the gristle over to the dogs and fed them one at a time, in size order. That's the way they ate in the wild. Biggest first. Feed them any other way and you're a dead man.

Then he hesitated. There were some funny noises. And Detroit felt the ground under them tremble. It wasn't an earthquake, it was—

"There's something burrowing under us," Detroit exclaimed.

They all stood, drawing their shotpistols. The ground exploded all around them. And out of the exploding gaps came hurtling snarling creatures. *Red-eyed, fanged creatures. They moved so fast they looked like blurs.*

One took a snap at Rock's heels; he shot it with his

pistol. "They're some sort of gopher," Rock said as another one jammed its jaws around his sleeve and tore off some material. Everyone had their hands full. The dogs thought it was great fun, for the creatures from the ground would bite at them, and then be slavered up by the big wolf-dogs, who didn't even bother to chew the foot-long creatures.

Chen tossed a series of knives, catching three of the hell-gophers in midair. The rest of the Freefighters fired wildly, but to some effect. The ravenous invaders had inch-long fangs; One got poor Danik on the right wrist and hung on trying to tear his arm off. Rock pushed the Eden citizen to the ground and stomped the brains out of the thing that wouldn't let go.

The humans weren't doing too well, but the sled dogs had broken loose and were having a field day chasing down the creatures. They closed their triple rows of teeth around them and swallowed them whole. Then a snarling gopher lunged for Scheransky's throat before he could fire. Class Act intervened. The intelligent female wolf-dog snapped the gopher out of midleap and digested it.

Because of the dogs, and only because of them, it was over. The dogs were sated, and fell asleep in a pile over by the scrubby Joshua trees. The humans dressed their wounds—Danik was the worst, but he was patched up and Chen gave him one of his potions. He'd be all right, Rock believed, they'd been lucky. Rock only found out later that half the supplies had been consumed by the furry devils!

"Do you think there are any more of them?" Danik asked, dry-mouthed. "Perhaps we'd better leave this cave . . ."

"You crazy?" McCaughlin said, "Go out in that temperature and wind in the middle of the night?"

"We'll post a guard," Rockson ordered. "I'll take first watch. Keep the fire high, sleep close to it. They shied from the fire—the holes in the ground are no closer than eight feet to the fire . . ."

"You're right," Rona exclaimed. "And besides, I think the dogs might have eaten 'em all—if not, they sure will eat any more that try that act again."

Scheransky went over and petted the furry head of Class Act. "I will never call you a mangy wolf again, I swear it by Lenin—I mean George Washington."

They had an uneasy night's sleep but there were no more incidents. Rock, between dozes, listened to the wind whistling by. It was as if it were speaking to him, warning him, "Go . . . home . . . Go . . . "

The next day the weather was better—overcast but not quite as cold, and they made good progress. Rockson said, "I believe what's left of Colorado Springs is right over that hill."

They came over the ridge and looked down on a glassy-surfaced blackened plain. "That's the area that took a nuke bomb hit back in the twentieth century," said Rockson grimly. "The heat of the air-detonated blast melted the sand into that shiny surface. Not a thing grows there to this day. You notice that there is no snow on that mile-wide plain either. There is still some heat from radioactive elements in that surface— hence the clicking you hear on the Geiger attached to the front of my sled. Let's give it some room."

"I remember this place," Danik said, "the President's Museum is about a mile away from here—just beyond those boulders shaped like a pile of kid's

61

blocks."

They quickly made for the boulderfield Danik had indicated. Rockson hoped that any roving scavengers attracted by the body of Run Dutil would not have eaten his notebook as well — some species of high-plains bobcat ate even metal cans!

The building was a two-story affair nestled in the midst of a flat area covered with snow — a parking lot of old. The big rocks had shielded it from the blast effects — everything else in these parts was flattened. It was partly collapsed. Danik was besides himself with feelings, and his voice was choked up when he said, "Through that second door — that's where my best friend and I stumbled frozen and hungry into the building."

Rockson and his Freefighters pulled up their sleds in front of the blackened crumbling structure and gingerly stepped into the ruin. It was dark inside; they lit a flashlight. Rockson gasped as his beam hit a human face. McCaughlin shouted, "Watch out — " and drew his shotpistol, before he realized the face was familiar.

"Well, I'll be a monkey's uncle. *Lincoln* — Abraham Lincoln — a plastic figure."

"His top hat don't look too good." Rona said. Indeed it didn't. There was a pack rat sticking its nose out of the decayed fabric.

"Let's move on," Rockson said.

Danik took the lead, and they passed a lifelike statue of Teddy Roosevelt riding a horse in the Battle of Bull Run, and then a replica of President Bush signing the Martial Law decree in the Oval Office. They finally came to the Rotunda Room. Light spilled in from above through a hole in the ceiling. The snow flurries drifted in on the figure of John F. Kennedy sitting in his rocking chair. He was staring forever at the three astronauts in spacesuits that had returned from the moon and were coming in to receive his accolades. A tattered and mouse-eaten American flag hung disintegrating on a pole nearby. JFK was up to his knees in snow.

"It wasn't like that when I was here two weeks ago," Danik gasped. "There was no hole in the roof."

"Do you think someone's been here?" McCaughlin said.

"No," Rock replied, "The weight of the snow finally got to the roof. Nothing lasts forever, not even the Hall of Presidents. Where is Run Dutil's body?"

"It should be over there—in the shadows—propped up against the wall. We found a steel box in here, all rusted and jammed closed. Some other hapless wanderers must have brought it here—we found disintegrating skeletons on the second floor, next to charred wood on a sheet-metal plate. When Run and I broke open the box, we found some canned goods inside. Must have been decades old, but we cut them open and ate the stuff. It tasted flat, but it wasn't spoiled. Canned Soviet-label meat. It gave me the strength to go on, but Run was sickening from a snake bite he got the sixth day out of Eden. He threw up the food and convulsed and died. I was—was too weak, delirious, frightened. I left him—and his notebook of our travels—right where he died." Danik's voice trailed off. He looked down.

Rockson shone the beam of his light over in the direction Danik indicated. The body was there, stiff and frozen, its eyes wide and mouth gaping, the lips

63

blue. Run Dutil looked a lot like Danik. The body appeared to be untouched; the cold had kept it from rotting. Perhaps the animals had tried to taste the plastic statues over the centuries and found them unpalatable. And so they had desisted from tasting this real human. Rockson fumbled through the dead man's clothing until he found the small steno pad with pencil notes inside an inner pocket of his frost-covered tunic.

Eagerly he played the light across its contents. "Direction readings," Rock yelled exhultantly. "Run Dutil took bearings and direction readings with a sextant. And there are some notes describing the places they stopped."

Detroit rummaged around and found the toy sextant Run Dutil had used for compiling his meager notes in JFK's plastic hands. It would be useful, for if the navigation device had some error in it, they could take that into account in plotting their trek south.

"Good work, Detroit," Rockson said. "We can try to reach Eden now!"

"Can we bury him?" Danik asked somberly.

Rockson wondered how they would spade the ground outside, seeing that it was frozen solid. Then he said, "We can roll some boulders over him—better that way—the animals can't get at him."

Danik agreed, Run Dutil was solemnly carried outside, still in his frozen, stiff sitting position. As McCaughlin rolled up good-sized rocks to the body and then hefted a capstone in place, Rockson said, "Ashes to ashes, dust to dust. Heavenly Father, we send you our friend Run Dutil, a good and true American. If you can see to do it, please welcome him into your arms. Amen."

They all chanted an amen in unison, and then went back and spread out their maps, and compared them to the notes from Run Dutil's little pad. Rockson drew some pencil marks on the maps, using the meager angles and sun-elevation heights that Dutil had jotted down. He drew estimated margin-of-error lines too— dotted lines that were as much as ten miles to one side or the other of their new route. Then they were off on their quest for Eden.

The dogs were howling and yapping, apparently happy to be on the trail again. They didn't like the President's museum much, it seemed.

Taking the bearing to the southeast that Dutil's notes indicated, they moved their sleds along at a good thirty miles per hour through icy weather conditions. Soon they were approaching the old border of Colorado into Arizona. But there was no letup in the cold temperatures, or in the golfball-sized hailstones pounding the hunched-down travelers.

# Chapter 8

They headed southward, guided by Run Dutil's notes in the little pad. Hopefully, they would find the next landmark on the route to Eden, the giant teepee that Danik had described.

Rockson needed every bit of his famed "mutant's luck" if they were to reach the obscure site. The bearing was vague, as Dutil had measured direction with a sextant that was little more than a toy.

They came upon an area 235 miles south of Colorado Springs Plain that Rockson himself had crossed years earlier. It was the area around a small hunter-trapper community called Moosehead. Moosehead Township was a set of ten or twelve wooden shacks and a tanning shed for hides. The Soviets usually ignored these primitive American communities, which served their purposes because their commanding officers did a brisk trade with the mountainmen who did fur trapping. Hides and furs were exchanged for rubles. The rubles bought the trapper families some precious supplies like salt in the small free markets in the shadows of the great Soviet forts further east.

But someone hadn't left Moosehead alone. When the Freefighters and their Edenite friend came within sight of the town, they started to see signs of destruction. Scattered along the red-stained snows were the bones of several animals—horse bones, dog bones, and what looked like a picked-clean small human arm bone.

"Wolves?" Rockson asked Detroit, pointing to the paw tracks all around the bones.

"The wolves *ate* the meat," said Detroit, "but see the bullet hole in this human femur?"

"Reds," Rona said, and drew her shotpistol.

Detroit nodded. "Probably. The animals came later—drawn by the blood."

"Let's get up on that hill and scan the area," Rock ordered. "Keep your weapons at the ready."

From the rise Rock could see that the shack-town beyond was a charred ruin. There were many bodies, some reduced to skeletons, wearing pieces of cloth the wolves didn't like the taste of. There were crates also, some six or seven feet wide. Putting down his binocs, Rock said, "The town was probably hit with artillery, and then mopped up by a squad of commandos." He swept the area again with his electron binoculars. "The fires are out; whatever happened occurred at least a day ago. Let's go down and see if we can find out why they hit it, and look for survivors."

Scheransky volunteered, "Maybe I should keep the sleds here, in case there's land mines, they're a bit hard to steer in exact situations. I can cover for you here, with my Dragunov sniper rifle, pick off anyone that comes near the town."

"Okay," Rock said. "You stay with the dog sleds. The rest of us go down and look around."

Scheransky slid the sniper rifle out of his sled's blankets and covered them, peering around the countryside far and wide through the telescopic sight. Then he left the rifle sitting on top of the blankets of his sled. He unzipped his parka. Crouching behind the sled he took out a small black box. It had lots of buttons on it. He pressed one. The box sprung to life with a dozen blinking lights. He seated it in the snow, and then pulled a whip antenna up to a height of three feet.

He left the device to do its secret work, then peered over the sled to make sure no one had turned back for some reason. The others must not know.

This was only the third time he'd had the opportunity to set up the device. If only they would leave him alone more, he could accomplish his job.

Rockson and his group skiied sullenly into the pathetic settlement's ruins. There were not only the bodies of adults, but children's half-eaten corpses too. And one little girl's frozen nude body had deep gashes in her pelvic area. She was hanging by the neck from a pole, swaying in the cold wind. Her anguished blank blue eyes stared at him as if — pleading for —

"McCaughlin, cut her down and bury her under some rocks," he ordered.

"Bastards," McCaughlin muttered as he worked. "Murdering bastards."

There were more bodies — ravaged women, men with missing testes, atrocities of all descriptions throughout the town. And lots of tracks of wolves.

But what attracted the Doomsday Warrior's attention most was the booted footprints of men. Soviet murderers' bootprints.

"What could they have done this for?" Danik asked softly of Detroit, who walked alongside, surveying the disaster site. "What did they want of these poor people?"

Rock had no reply.

The tanning shack was partly standing. The team headed that way. Rock told Danik to stand guard outside the shack. He put a shotpistol into his thin long hand. "Better get used to holding this baby."

Entering the shack with Liberator rifles set on full auto, just in case, the search team found a man. He was trussed up by a rope on the one unfallen central wood beam. He was still alive, and he moaned when he saw them.

The survivor was not a pretty sight. Rock instinctively shielded Rona's eyes, then withdrew his hand. Who was he kidding? The woman had been in the middle of the worst action a dozen times. She had seen as bad, and worse.

The man had one eye half pulled from its bloody socket; his lips were cracked and blue from the cold. He wore a torn fur parka lanced with a hundred bloody holes—perhaps the short jabs of a Soviet cavalry bayonet, sunk deep enough to make the man talk and talk. Torture. His one good eye tracked Rock as he approached.

"I don't know," the agonized man pleaded. "Please, kill me, don't hurt me anymore."

"No one's gonna hurt you," the Doomsday Warrior said softly. He gave the man a drink from his canteen.

70

He was about to cut him down, when he saw that the man was just a torn mass inside his clothing. The guts of the man had been pulled out of a hole in his stomach. Slippery coils of intestines pulsed with pain. To move him . . .

"The Reds did this?"

The man nodded slightly. "They—they wanted information on—on—some modern-dressed stranger they picked up on their instruments. They said they knew he was near here. One of their automatic overflight drones—Midnight Marauders—detected him. That was about—few days ago . . . Thought he might be a Free—Freefighter, 'cause he was dressed—different then us simple folk. I—we—told them we didn't see—didn't know . . . they shot our children one by one, trying to find out—but God, we didn't—"

Rockson knew injuries—when they were hopeless, when they weren't. This was hopeless. The man had minutes. His trussed hands were blue swollen dead things, the circulation out of them for hours. The man's lips trembled, spoke these words: "Please, please . . . kill me. Kill me—"

Rockson lifted his shotpistol and dispatched the man from his agony. "We'll bury him too—alongside the little girl," Rockson said. "We can't stop to collect all the bones in this town, but we will bury the two of them as a token of respect for all the people martyred here."

On the way to the pile of rocks at the edge of town that would serve as the burial site, the Freefighters came upon two dead Russians. Their faces were eaten away by the wolves, but their uniforms of cheap brown synthetic material hadn't proved as tasty. "A lieutenant and a sergeant," Rock noted, pointing to the stripes on their sleeves. "There's a bullet hole in each of their heads — big caliber."

The Sov's guns were out. Tokarev ten-shot pistols. Fired.

Behind the rocks the Freefighters found the American shooter's body. A mountain man with a blunder-buss single-shot moose gun. He was intact; the wolves had been busy on the Sovs.

"We'll bury this brave and good man too. He deserves it."

As they returned to Scheransky, who had been watching them with the binoculars as they made their grim rounds, Danik asked about the shot in the shed. Rockson told him they had found a man in pain, but alive. Beyond help.

"Did you find out why the Reds did this?" Danik asked. "I know from the tapes I studied in Century City that a community like this is usually left alone . . ."

Rockson saw no point in telling Danik that *he* was the unwitting cause of this atrocity. "No, we don't know why the Reds did this," Rock said flatly. "We have to move on."

It was always their intention to save the precious food supply the carried for themselves and hunt food for the wolf-dog teams. But they'd seen no game, not even any tracks, since setting out. Now, when they did see tracks, it was that of a small rabbit.

The tracks were hours old, Rock saw when he

stooped to examine them. "No sense in going after the little thing; it would hardly sate the teams anyway. Let's push on," Rock said. "I don't like the looks of those clouds." He pointed up to the south.

"More acid snow?" Rona asked.

"No, but nevertheless it's sure to be a bad storm."

Indeed in a matter of minutes a wind started rising and soon became a howling enemy. The wind-driven snow, though of the ordinary variety, took their breaths away. It was coming directly from the south, so the choice was either to take a different tack or fight it. Rockson compromised, ordering the team to turn southwest and keep moving.

The temperature dropped rapidly. Rock glanced at the thermometer reading on his watch — seventy below. He saw Danik falter and let go of his rope and fall. Rock stopped the sleds. McCaughlin raced over and helped Rock put the man on his sled, covering him with everything available.

"What's wrong with him?" McCaughlin asked, shouting into the wind.

"I think he's still a bit weak from his ordeal getting to Century City. All the vitamin shots in the world can't make up for a frozen trek like that. The Edenites never had to endure much in the way of low temperatures. We've got to find shelter." Rock replied.

To make things worse, in another ten minutes of slow travel, the dogs abandoned their fanned-out position at the end of the nylon rope traces and tangled themselves into immobility. They began howling and biting at the strong rope. "We've got to untangle them, find shelter," Rock implored.

It took twenty minutes of bone-chilling work for

all of them to untangle the dogs—and they had to take off their mittens to straighten out the traces. They were well on their way to having frostbitten fingers by the time they got moving again. Danik was barely conscious, bundled down under ten layers of blankets and furs in Rockson's sled.

They were on a high plateau, totally exposed to the elements. Rock had to find them cover *now*, or Danik would die. And the mission with him.

Rockson took up the infrared binoculars and scanned ahead. The binocs cut through some of the obscuring effects of the storm. Dimly Rockson made out a line of boulders ten or twelve miles ahead, down from their exposed position on the hill, in a little valley. Maybe there would be shelter somewhere in that jumble of rocks. He certainly hoped so.

The Doomsday Warrior, lifting the many fur coverings, took a glance at Danik's face. It was ashen, his breathing was shallow. He hoped he would last till they got there.

It took another twenty minutes to get into the sheltered valley and find a group of three huge rocks. There was a space between the them big enough for the humans to scramble through with their tent and some supplies—including the Primus stove.

Danik had to be passed from arms to arms wrapped in his blankets, for he was completely unconscious. There was just enough room to set up the survival tent there among the boulders out of the wind. With frozen determination, they accomplished that task, and pulled the stove inside and lit it up. They placed Danik closest to the stove's heat. The dogs would manage in the lee of the wind, sleeping in a huge tumble with one another. They had the stamina to do so.

There in the rapidly erected silver tent the cold and hungry Freefighters huddled. As the tent slowly grew warmer, they began to unpack the bundle of foodstuffs Rock had dragged along. Danik came around as the temperature rose. They fed him some hot broth McCaughlin brewed up out of chunks of preserved venison, some melted snow, and vitamin capsules.

They were safe from Mother Nature's winter wrath. For now.

The alarm woke him up at six o'clock; McCaughlin eased out among them. It was totally dark. It shouldn't be. No—there was a bit of light at the very peak of the tent. He realized they were nearly buried in snow. The Scots-American rose up to full height; the air was *very* stale. He snapped open the chimney slit in the tent top. It instantly got colder, but the air was okay. He peered through the hole. It had stopped snowing—they could dig out later. The others began to stir.

McCaughlin knew what was needed besides his jokes to restore morale. He started up breakfast: venison strips as bacon substitute and hot coffee and biscuits—the kind you just put in a pan and swell up once you cover them and they steam. His own famous trail biscuits.

Sniffing the food odors did more to awaken his companions than did the alarm. "Rise and shine, mateys, breakfast is all ready."

"Never heard a more pleasant sentence," Rockson

said. He turned up the Coleman lamp and looked around at the bundled-up Freefighters now coming to life. "Why is it so dark in here?"

McCaughlin explained. Rock frowned. "Of course—how could I be so stupid—we could have suffocated."

"Not with you along we couldn't," McCaughlin said. "You have mutant's luck, remember?"

Danik lay half asleep still on Rockson's sled when they set off on their way again. He was still the worse for wear, but improving rapidly after the warmth and sleep and good food. The warming sunbeams seemed to bring the man around further.

Rockson took sun readings every three hours, when they paused for hot green tea—an Eskimo custom Rock had picked up.

Scheransky asked Rockson to come to look at some odd ice formations a bit away from the others. He had something, he said, on his mind. Rockson asked him what it was.

Scheransky's dark eyes were intense. "I want to know what really happened to you out in the desert, after our Alaska mission last year. After you left us in Alaska to chase down that missile; what happened to you? What's the big secret about the missing five days of your trek to Century City? I heard that the only one you told is Dr. Schecter."

Rockson decided to tell Scheransky. He was a technician, a scientist. Perhaps someone other than Schecter *should* know. Maybe Scheransky could help Schecter in his project, a project based upon what

76

had happened in Rockson's missing five days. "I went backward in time, that's what happened."*

"Backward in time? Is that possible?"

"I didn't believe it was—but it happened. I was caught in a twin-tornado storm—one of the *Kala-Ka* storms you've probably read about. I was tossed through some sort of time portal, and went back to 1989. I'll tell you sometime what happened back there. The important thing is I came back into the present. Schecter thinks that it would be theoretically possible to set up the same conditions I encountered in the *Kala-Ka* artificially in the lab and send me—or someone—back in time again. It would be very dangerous . . ."

"Then, why—"

"Scheransky, think a second. What could you, what would *you* do in 1989, if you could?"

"Back in 1989? Why, that's when—"

"Right—that's when World War Three started. If someone were to go back in time and, say, assassinate Premier Drushkin—the man who launched the surprise attack on America—"

Scheransky gasped. "Why, then the war would never—"

"Right. The war might never have happened. America wouldn't have been devastated. There wouldn't have been the death of billions of men, women, and children; the radiation clouds wouldn't have swept over the planet."

The Russian sank back on his heels. "*Da*. But that

*See Doomsday Warrior #10.

might have some — unpleasant consequences. It would change *everything*. Even who is alive in the twenty-first century. It would change history so much. There would never be a Century City, for instance."

"You see the problem. Very good. *If* and it's a big if — *if* Schecter can accomplish time travel, it would be a better idea to change things just *slightly*, so that — say — the Reds' occupation of America after the war was not very successful. Or perhaps go back and take out just the Soviet missiles that went off track and hit our nuclear power plants — and sent all that radiation up into the air. Something like that would be better than undoing all of history."

Scheransky whistled. "That would be tremendous."

"Of course, it's only theoretically possible. And if the Russians were to get the gist of what I just told you, they could start research on the *Kala-Ka* phenomenon on their own and perhaps also achieve time travel. That's why only Schecter — and now you — know."

"Oh, my god. This *must not* get to the Soviets."

"Yes . . . you see the problem. Now you understand why it's top-top-secret."

"I swear by my mother's grave . . ."

"I know, Scheransky, I know. Now I told you because I think with your technical background, with what you know about Soviet technology, you might be able to lend Schecter a hand with the project, once we get back . . ."

"I would love nothing better, my friend."

"Good. I'll see to it. Now that I let the cat out of the bag with you, I can't see Schecter not bringing

78

you in on it. It would take some of the enormous burden off his shoulders to have an assistant."

"You honor me, my friend. And I am so happy that you trust me . . ."

Rockson squeezed his shoulder. "I trust you totally. You're a part of the team. You're one of us now."

# Chapter 9

They made good time trekking, covering a hundred winding miles through rolling terrain each day. They camped in snow caves or rock overhangs. The routine set in. Up at dawn, check the dogs, feed them a ration portion each of the dwindling dried meat supply, get some breakfast down themselves, then drive the teams across the deep winter snow. Tea and pemmican breaks in the trek, navigation readings and comparing the notebook and their maps. And always, always, tugging at Rockson's gut, the realization that they could be hopelessly off course.

Six days after the Hall of Presidents, they found evidence of game. Deer tracks.

They braked their sleds, drew them behind some winterberry bushes, as a wind shield.

Archer was the first to volunteer. "Meeee gooo huntttt," he demanded. He drew up his huge make-shift crossbow and a four-foot barbed steel arrow, which he notched. "Ookayyy?"

Rockson thought a bit, then said, "No, old fellow. We need you to watch over the teams. The dogs love you. We can't handle them without you near."

Archer's chest swelled. "Meee goooddd," he stated, and he pounded on his chest so loud it sounded like a bass drum.

"Thanks, pal, I knew I could count on you."

Rockson considered their ad hoc camp a good one. Behind winterberry brambles; a natural shield of thorns.

"Rona and I will use some arrows and get the venison," he promised.

Rockson took up his compound bow — a plastic and steel marvel of engineering with a hundred-ninety-pound pull. "Ready, Rona?" She had her bow on her shoulder. "Sure, lead on."

Rock wanted Rona as backup. Rock had to admit she was equal to him in skill if not in sheer power of draw. He couldn't afford to miss. And firearms were out. No sense alerting any chance Soviet patrol.

Three hours of trekking and the couple was in sight of the eight-point buck and his doe. The problem was getting *downwind* from the gentle creatures nuzzling on the evergreen branches.

It took *another* hour for Rockson and Rona to get in position in the boulderfield directly north of the pair of deer. Rockson carefully notched his arrow and let fly the shot at the buck, but the stag had suddenly started.

There was a movement in the narga grass — and one of Post-nuke America's plethora of wildswine appeared. The supersensitive snout of the beast stuck high into the air. The four-tusked three-hundred-pound beast snorted. It had caught the scent of the two Freefighters.

"Damn," said Rona as the alerted deer darted away, jumping into the copse of trees. "There goes our venison steaks."

"How about some pork chops," Rockson said angrily, swiveling his bow and letting loose a good shot at the spoiler of their hunt.

But the wildswine had suddenly darted sideward with a sharp squeal. The super-swift porker, a dangerous crossbreed of wild Asian swine and the domestic hog of the twentieth century, also avoided the frying pan.

"*Shit,*" Rock said, reaching into his quiver and taking out another steel-tipped arrow. He notched it and said, "The pig is over in that jumble of rocks— let's get it. Rona, you go around the other way. We'll have pork tonight, or my name isn't Ted Rockson."

But as the couple gradually, silently moved to encircle the wild swine, there was a sudden shaking of the ground. Rock swiveled on his heels to see a giant version of the swine he was stalking tear through a copse of trees the size of telephone poles, knocking them down like toothpicks. The thing was a pig—but it stood twelve or thirteen feet at its shoulders and was at least twice that length. It stopped in its tracks, snorted a twin stream of hot steam out of its flaring nostrils. And then it turned its ugly snout directly in the direction of Rockson and roared out a challenge.

Rona and Rock let fly their arrows, each hitting one of the beast's huge eyes. But the arrows just bounced. "Rona—head for cover in the rocks, I'll lead it away." With that admonition, the twenty-first-century warrior took off at a lope. The giant swine started pawing the ground; it lowered its head like a bull. Then it took off after him, like a freight train chasing a stray cat.

"Rock," Rona yelled, "be careful."

Rockson *was* being careful. He had made for a second outcropping of sharper, tumbled rocks, and now dove in among the boulders, rolled into a crevice. He removed his shotpistol from his holster and took the the safety off. Just in time. The giant swine screeched to a stop and leaned its steamy snout down into Rock's hiding place. Its huge tongue licked down at the Doomsday Warrior. Naturally, he fired. Point-blank.

The lower incisors and molars of the beast exploded into chalky fragments tinged with red, and the X-pattern of explosive pellets peppered the sinewy red throat beyond. But the thing didn't die. It pulled back, startled by the blast. Then it charged against the rocks, almost burying Rockson in a shifting mass of granite. He managed to extricate himself and, not anxious to be buried in the next attack, he took off again. Rockson was firing over his shoulder when the opportunity presented itself. Two of his frantic shots hit dead center in the snout of the beast, sending out sprays of nostril meat and blood, but it just sneezed and then continued the chase.

The shotpistol empty, Rock flung it back; the beast swallowed it without changing pace. Rockson spotted Rona a hundred feet ahead, running fast, but not as fast as Rockson, and he soon caught up to her. "Pour it on, girl," he gasped out, "I couldn't stop it."

"Rock, how about my smoke bombs?"

"Smokebombs? Hell, use them, Rona, quickly."

Rona was already reaching into her belt pouch. She

84

tossed a handful of the small glass cylinders behind her. The *pop-pop-pop* of the shattering glass was music to Rockson's ears. The thundering hoofs of their immense pursuer stopped. There was a great cloud of putrid-smelling black smoke behind the two runners now. An enormous sneeze reverberated in the cold air. Imagine what that stuff smells like to its sensitive nostrils, Rock thought. That ought to stop him for a while.

But a while was a mere five or six seconds. Enough for the Freefighters to gain a hundred feet, but then the terrible thundering hoofs started coming again.

Rockson could see the tangle of brambles that he hoped was the encampment wall ahead. He yelled, "Freefighters, set the Liberator rifles on full automatic, we've got supper coming up behind us — don't spare the gunpowder."

Rockson's rear end was now less than twenty feet ahead of the razor-sharp tusks.

# Chapter 10

"Did you hear that?" McCaughlin said, snapping up from where he crouched feeding another stick into the low campfire. "Look, over there!"

Detroit saw where he was pointing, and heard more clearly what Rockson was yelling. "Quick," Detroit exclaimed, "Aim high, don't hit our friends. *Shoot!*"

Frantically they lifted their rifles. Chen, wanting accuracy, set down his tripod mount for steadiness atop the small rise; they all fired on full auto at the beast.

The big guns spoke a thousand throaty words. The simple statement could not be ignored. It said, "Death to big pigs."

A shuddering series of impacts on the pig knocked it to the ground. Splattered pieces of smoking meat and shards of bone matter flew over Rock and Rona as they dove over the brambles to their friends. All the Freefighters' uniforms were coated with a rain of red blood. A pulsing bit of pig brain-matter splashed into Scheransky's hands as he tried to cover his face. Rockson, too, was thoroughly reddened by the rain of blood. They kept firing for a while—just in case!

Rona jumped across the hollow, and grabbed the Doomsday Warrior into her arms. "Oh, you great big hunk of a man," she said, kissing his red-stained face over and over—everywhere. "You saved me. You lured the thing to you, you did it to save me."

When she finally let go, Rockson smiled, "Not exactly. I wanted pork chops for supper, that's all."


Before the roaring cooking fire had died to red coals in the early darkness, the smell of roast pork spread through the valley. The fattiest meat was given to the ravenous wolf-dogs, who had endured so much and gotten them over eight hundred miles already. The Rock Team went to their sleeping bags with a warm glow in their bellies—especially after the Scot passed around his Glenlivet. "It's a hundred and six years old, laddies, so don't ye spill a drop."

"Now, that's *old* scotch." Detroit said, swigging down a large portion. Danik had a restorative slug too.

"Save some for the Russkies," said Scheransky, taking the bottle. "I prefer vodka, but defectors can't be choosers. I'll make do." He too took a swig. And so did the rest of them. Rona finished it off in two glugs, and wiped her mouth, tossed the bottle into the brush.

"Now, *that's* a woman you got there, Rock," said McCaughlin.


The next day's trek was an uneventful passage over

gently rolling snow under pink cirrus clouds. Rockson, stopping the group at midafternoon, used the navigation devices that Schecter had provided, and also used the toy sextant that Dutil had figured angles and distance with. He announced that they were well out on the rolling plains of Arizona. Some divine power must, they reasoned, be favoring their quest.

The citizen of Eden had been extraordinarily quiet. He was sitting up on Rock's sled, watching the scenery go by. Rock, hoping he wasn't getting sick again, spoke to him. "You all right, Danik?"

"Wonderful. It's so beautiful, that's why I'm quiet. This land is so beautiful. What is there to say in the face of such beauty?"

"I guess we Americans take for granted the majesty of the countryside, Danik. It's a good thing someone comes along once in a while to tell us what we have. So we notice it more. So we appreciate it. You know it was all almost completely destroyed a hundred and five years ago — when the two superpowers fired their ICBMs at one another. The ignorant bastards almost destroyed it all."

"Stafford plans to finish their evil handiwork — make this beautiful world a no-man's land," Danik said sadly. "I hope we can stop him. God, I pray that we can stop him."

After nearly one hundred miles more, all against a fierce icy wind, the party of bold adventurers were beginning to doubt the directions given by the notebook. They should have reached the next landmark — the tall teepee-shaped building.

89

Still, there was nothing to do but go on.

They were ten miles further along than the notebook indicated, and all were depressed and feeling hopeless, when Danik himself shouted the good news: "There it is, the whale rock. We are on the right track."

"Thank God Run Dutil's notes were accurate at least to the direction, if not to the distance," Rock uttered with relief.

Recalculating their path taking into account the navigational error of two degrees and ten miles, Rockson headed the bone-weary squad off again to the south. And after two more hard hours fighting winds and driven snow, they came upon a crumbling highway town. There in the middle of the rust spots in the snow that had been Buicks and Toyotas and Oldsmobiles over a hundred years ago, was the giant teepee. It had the look of a new building. "We buried two companions behind it," Danik said softly.

"It must be some sort of plastic," Rockson said. "Plastic lasts longer than concrete. Keep the dogs back, Detroit, come with me; I want to make sure no one is in there. It looks so spiffy, I don't trust it."

The team members held their sleds back behind some tumbled boulders, and Rock and the bull-necked black Freefighter walked cautiously forward, guns drawn, inspecting the many windows in the five-story bright-orange-and-yellow "teepee" for any movements. "Keep an eye on that mesa behind the building," Rockson said. "There's a thousand places a man with a rifle could hole up in those rocks." Detroit nodded.

The sign over the door, a ten-foot-high red plastic

affair, said TOMAHAWK INDIAN STORE, save now, 50% off Indian Jewelry."

"Good, we're in time for the sale," Detroit whisperingly joked.

Rockson and Detroit cautiously entered the giant replica of an Indian dwelling. Light sifted in from outside through high windows. Tumbled chairs, smashed tables, precious items of beaten silver and turquoise—necklaces, rings, bracelets—lay unmolested in glass cases. But other glass counters by the rusty cash register were smashed. "They kept candy by the register," Rock said, holstering his shotpistol, "In the weeks after the nuke war, any kind of food was precious—much more precious than jewelry." A quick survey found the place uninhabited.

It was a good place to stay for the night, for there was an old Franklin stove actually still in one piece. They gathered firewood—smashing the dried wooden counters of the soda fountain for fuel. Soon the immense teepee had blue-white smoke coming out its top, and the Freefighters and the man from Mexico were sitting around eating their pemmican and pork stew. McCaughlin, the official morale builder, began playing his harmonica. They sang a few choruses of "Jimmy Crack Corn," and a few patriotic songs like "America the Beautiful." That brought tears to Danik's eyes. Then they all bedded down and fell into a well-deserved warm and cozy sleep.

Scheransky carefully slipped from his sleeping bag in the dead of night and nearly soundlessly stole away from the company of exhausted Freefighters. Before he moved off into the crescent-moon-lit darkness outside the odd building, the Russian reached into a pack on his sled and took out the small black-box device. It fit right into the palm of his hand.

Sure that no one had noticed his awakening, he slipped away into the snowy darkness.

But someone had noticed. Chen. Though as tired as the others, Chen's martial arts training allowed him to sleep lightly when on a mission, and to unconsciously note any unusual noise. He opened his brown-amber eyes and without the slightest movement of his head or body tracked the silent Russian defector. Then, as stealthily as the Russian had moved, Chen rose and followed. At the doorway he saw Scheransky go behind some boulders.

What was the Russian up to? Chen couldn't believe he was up to something bad. Maybe it was just a call of nature that drove Scheransky over the ridge? What if it wasn't? Chen had bought the Russian's story of believing in the American cause. Chen had believed — up until this point — that Scheransky was a true and loyal American Freefighter now. He certainly had honored himself in the Alaska mission, and Rockson trusted Scheransky implicitly.

But then *where the hell* was he going? As Chen stalked him over the ridge of boulders, he saw Scheransky now running in the distance. The man was certainly not just taking a piss. No, he *was* up to something.

Chen shot from boulder to boulder. The Russian never looked back to see if he was being followed. He stopped suddenly and put a device in his hand down and pulled out an antenna. He started pushing on it—buttons perhaps.

A transmitter of some kind, Chen concluded. The Soviet defector must not be a defector at all—he must be giving away their position. He should throw a stardart—kill the man he had come to trust as a friend over the past months— *No!* He hesitated.

Chen put the shuriken back into his belt pouch. He instead ran like lightning, silently as a deer, at the Russian kneeling there in the snow. Chen jumped him just as he was turning, having heard the faint crunch of snow.

*Wham*, Chen was upon him. The Russian fought like a madman but Chen had him tied up in knots with a reverse hammerhold and his face half buried in the snow, his arms twisted violently behind him. Scheransky, for the first time *seeing* his silent attacker, exclaimed, "Chen, it's *you*."

"Yes, you bastard. It's me. What are you doing?"

"Ease up, Chen, you're hurting me."

"Not until you tell me what you're doing!" Chen saw now that the device had a number of small blinking red lights on it. The antenna waved in the arctic-like wind. Scheransky tried again to struggle out of Chen's grip, but to no avail.

"*Talk*, you traitor—or I'll break your arm."

Scheransky spat out snow and said, "All right, all right. It's an—experiment—for—for Dr. Schecter."

"Oh yeah? Then, how come we're not in on it?" Chen tightened his twist of the Russian's arm.

"Ow, let go, let go."

"Let him go, Chen," said a voice from behind. Chen turned to see Rockson's cleated boots near his face. And Rona and Archer too were coming up

93

behind him. "Caught him with this device," Chen said, pushing Scheransky's device across the snow with his foot. "Take a look." He let the Russian sit up. Scheransky started rubbing his shoulder. He leaned over to retrieve his black-box device.

"Stay away from that device," Rock said, unholstering his pistol.

"Don't worry, I will," said Scheransky, withdrawing his hand.

"Now, what's this about?"

Scheransky sighed. "You're not supposed to know."

"Tell me anyway."

"I never trusted him," Chen offered. "A Red is a Red."

"Tell me," Rockson said again, cocking his shotpistol.

"Oh shit, Rock," Scheransky said, "its an experiment for Dr. Schecter. He wants—wants to m-measure the atmospheric changes that have brought on this terrible winter—the worst since the war."

Rockson went over and crouched next to the device. He saw after careful inspection that it was not a transmitter. Still it *was* an electronic device. And Rockson had specifically forbidden the bringing along of any electronic devices because the Russians had a way of homing in on them.

"Do you believe me? Here—here," said the Russian, taking out a crumpled note. "Here is the letter from Dr. Schecter explaining—in case I was seen using the device . . ."

Rockson read:

*To Ted Rockson, This is to advise you that I have overridden your objection to any electronic devices being brought along on your mission. I have done this with the full support of Rath and the council. Scheransky was told by the council that he had to obey. The data being collected is of vital importance. Sorry for the subterfuge.*

*Dr. Schecter.*

He passed the note around. Chen sighed exasperatedly, pulled Scheransky up from the snow, and said, "Do you realize I was about to blow you to kingdom come with an explosive star-dart when I saw you take out the device?"

Scheransky, brushing the snow from his parka, said, "I'm glad you didn't."

Rockson said, "Well, collect the damned information and let's get back to some shuteye."

"Yes, can a person get an uninterrupted night of sleep around here?" demanded Rona. "You guys are worse than the gobble-gophers for losing a girl her beauty sleep."

Rockson, putting his arm over Scheransky's shoulder as they crunched back to camp in the snow, said he would think over whether or not Scheransky could continue with the data collection.

In the morning, over coffee and dried pemmican, Rockson said, "Scheransky, go ahead. Keep collecting Schecter's damned data. By the way—why did you go so far from camp to do it?"

"If—if the electronic pulses were picked up by an enemy patrol—I wanted to be the only one who was caught . . ." He looked down at his coffee.

95

Chen went over and said, "And to *think* I distrusted you."

"Okay," said Rock, breaking the guilt-ridden mood, "If anyone *else* has any wild surprises I'd appreciate hearing about it now—otherwise, let's pack up and get on our way."

The notebook gave the direction to the mysterious elegant bridge as southeast, two hundred twelve miles away. Rock spent hours of the smooth, level run wondering what the hell a giant stone bridge could be doing out here, going no place, on a shallow lake. He couldn't wait to solve the mystery.

After hours of speeding along—it was practically a race—came some rougher going. A twisting, narrow canyon.

Rockson ordered that the sled teams be driven in one at a time, spaced about a hundred yards apart. There were many feet of snow piled at the tops of those precipitous cliffs on both sides; the slightest noise could bring an avalanche. Yet there was no break in the cliffs save this canyon as far as their electron binocs could scan. They'd have to chance it.

Rock, Chen, and Archer would drive the sleds through. Archer first, hopefully settling the dogs down, informing them in his subtle ways that they must not howl or bark or make any noises. Then the remaining four Freefighters would ski through. The danger wouldn't be as great for them.

It was as good a plan as he could devise.

Rock watched as Archer made the first entry into the narrow orifice, he and the sled disappearing in the

96

shadowed turns of the canyon. He sighed, and whispered a "Mush." His own team took off after their big mountain man-buddy. Rockson winced each time he heard a creak of a sled or a half-whine from the dogs, who sensed, he was sure, the danger.

In the dark narrow canyon, he found a profound *closeness* to death—*and* to the Creator. He never caught sight of Archer's sled until he exited the canyon.

Rock breathed a sigh of relief to plunge into bright sunlight; another day of *life*. Both the Doomsday Warrior and Archer watched the canyon exit anxious for the safety of Chen.

Chen took a long time to appear, but finally they saw his lead dogs huffing and puffing their way to safety. Chen waved.

Next came the skiers, also paced a hundred yards apart. Detroit, then McCaughlin, Scheransky . . . But where was Rona?

Anxious minutes went by. Rona didn't appear. A cloud went across the sun; Rockson detected a wind coming up. He said, "I'm going back in after her . . ." He was about to set off when she appeared waving, shouting, "Hey, here I am. Sorry I'm late, but there was this *great* snowflower, I picked . . ." She waved a purple blossom over her head.

There were stirrings in the canyon as her echo coursed through it. Then a tremendous *whumpp*. She skiied up to them as a giant billowing white cloud exited the canyon.

*Close*.

Danik, when they reached the next rise, informed them, "See that blue mesa ahead, wreathed in clouds? I remember that one. Ten or so miles beyond it lies the bridge."

After traversing the distance to the mesa, cutting around its towering granite, they were immersed in a wet fog. Slowly they advanced their teams until Danik shouted, "There it is."

A parting in the fog bank revealed, straddled over a calm lake, amidst some low buildings and many bare trees, a bridge.

"My God, that's *London Bridge,*" Rock exclaimed.

Detroit said incredulously, "London Bridge? How can that be? Wasn't it in London when they nuked the place?"

Rockson and the Freefighters couldn't believe their eyes — a long, elegant many-arched stone bridge crossed the gentle waters of a desert lake. And it looked exactly like London Bridge, as they had seen many times in history books.

Rockson smacked his forehead and said, "I remember reading that some millionaire bought the whole bridge, and shipped it over to Arizona — that was when the Brits needed money badly. A few decades before World War Three. No one in Century City knows where the bridge was sent and reconstructed. Until now. Here it is."

"Why take London Bridge to Arizona? Did they need a bridge that bad?"

"I think I remember reading that some entrepreneur type thought it would be a good tourist attraction."

"And so the mystery of the bridge to nowhere is

solved." Danik said. "My companions—the two that died here—are entombed behind one of the big rocks in the bridge foundation. The mortar was cracked and weak. I and my surviving friends thought it would be a good grave."

Rockson and the others whipped their dogs up to traverse the distance to the spot Danik indicated. There were still signs of the massive bridge foundation rock, at the edge of the water, having been removed and replaced.

"A good place," Detroit said. "We will not disturb them."

Rockson and the team came upon a fallen, rust-pocked sign, lifted it. It said, "Welcome to London Bridge, Havasu City Arizona."

"You're right, Rock," Rona said, "You sure are a history buff."

Rockson frowned. "We have only one problem now—which way from here to Eden?"

Danik said, "Doesn't the notebook show?"

"I didn't want to tell anybody this—but," Rockson admitted, "the notebook didn't start until Dutil started writing it after he saw this bridge. He found the toy sextant here in a—let's see . . ." Rockson flipped through the pages. "Here it is, he found the sextant in 'Ye olde nautical gift shoppe.' There, right next to the bridge."

"Then," Rona said despondently, "we have no way of finding Eden."

"Yes, we do," Danik shouted exultantly. "Returning here, seeing the tomb of my friends did something—I can remember—not a lot, but something."

"*What?*" Rock asked, with great emotion.

"I remember that the first week we traveled, the week that brought us this far, cold and hungry and with two of us deathly sick, was all spent traveling directly north . . ."

"Following the North Star," Rock said, remembering Danik's tale. "Yes, I followed the North Star on the clear nights. We found shelter and slept in the slightly warmer days. I know that we came directly from the south of here."

Rockson said, "Great. We'll set out as soon as we take a look around here — for the record. And to see if anyone was here first. We might not be the only people seeking Eden," he said darkly.

They went into the gift shoppe and, because there were few windows, lit a Coleman lamp. Rock seated himself at a table, the Freefighters and Danik gathered around him. He unfolded the detailed topographical map the Freefighter carried. It was ancient, drawn on the basis of satellite photographs from the twentieth century.

"Now we know where we are, and we know—" he said, drawing his finger down south of the U.S.-Mexican border, "approximately where we are going. A week's walking distance is about — *here*."

Rock's finger had traced down to the San Piedro mountain range.

"Danik might remember some landmarks if we can get him close to the mountains that Eden is hidden in. So we head south to, say, the tallest mountain in the range."

"Mt. Obispo?" Rona asked.

"With a stopover at Yumak City — to retire these sleds and wolf-dogs. It's a good thing Yumak City is only a slight diversion from our route to Mt. Obispo. Look here—" Rock traced his finger south about seventy miles and then east for twenty. "See? Not so great a detour. I hope there's enough snow on the ground to allow us to get there without lugging everything by foot."

"We could make some sort of wagon." Detroit said.

"We have to hurry. I think there will be enough snow. I hope so. Let's get going." He folded the map. "First, Yumak City, our resupply point; then on to Mt. Obispo. And keep your collective fingers crossed," Rock said.

# Chapter 11

Meanwhile in Eden, Coronation Day had arrived . . .

The orchestra was all brass, no strings, no drums. The instruments were badly corroded, not having been used in a hundred years. Nobody knew how to play them either, but that didn't matter. Nobody in Eden knew what music was supposed to sound like, or exactly what it was for. The founder—in all his wisdom—had forgotten to store any music in the vaults of Eden. The inhabitants knew that music was important to have on momentous occasions. And they did their best to recreate the concept from what they remembered of their grandparents' humming tunes.

The music played by the one-hundred-man marching orchestra was a cacophonous rendition of "God Save the King." People plugged their ears with their fingers as the marching band passed. Then they bowed their heads as the only car in Eden—a 1989 red Ford Fiesta—crawled by with the window rolled down in the rear and the king-to-be Charles Stafford waved and nodded.

The end of the parade was made up of thirty

bulldozers, two abreast, also fouling the limited air with their dioxides.

Everyone in the city had lined the parade route to view the inaugural parade—for it was not wise to miss the show. It would appear that they didn't respect and adore their new leader-for-life. And to oppose meant to die.

King Charles, for his part, was pleased with the way things were going. He stepped out of the car when it reached the Government Building to appropriate *oohs* and *aaahs* from the public. And why not? He was wearing a vermilion satin robe encrusted with 1000 five- to ten-carat diamonds that glinted in the spotlight especially arranged to be trained upon his gleaming body at that precise moment. Vainly he smiled, then turned to walk up the twenty-one steps to the throne that was waiting for him at the top of the stairs. The orchestra below raged and fretted with their untuned instruments in an attempt to make up with noise for what they lacked in musicianship, for their lack of knowledge on how to play the tubas, trombones, and trumpets they held to their bleeding lips.

"Where is my crown?" Stafford said, annoyed. He sat down. His personal servant Mannerly came running with the vermilion pillow upon which rested the newly constructed crown. The only model the craftsmen had for such a thing was an old wallet-sized depiction of Jesus, who was reputed to be, by legend, some sort of king. They had thus constructed the gold and jewel crown in the shape of a crown of thorns, and realizing it would be difficult to wear, had lined the sharper points with plastic buttons. It gleamed in the spotlight also.

"Crown me, Mannerly," Stafford said.

The bleating of the maniac brass reached new heights of shrilldom as the servant leaned over and did just that. The coronation was over.

Nobody knew what to do, they all waited for their new king to tell them. But he just sat there smiling. Several of the orchestra players—all rather pale and emaciated—collapsed, noses and lips bleeding from the strain of their frantic playing.

Finally, as the wind went out of more and more of the mad musicians, until only a whimpering trumpet carried on, Stafford arose. He lifted his hand in a blessing and said, "From this day forth it is retroactively illegal to have disagreed with me. Treasonable thoughts are illegal, and any opposition is treason, punishable by death, Amen."

"Amen," yelled the populace.

"We tried democracy and it just didn't work," said Stafford, once the amens had died down, "It is time for the entertainment I promised you all. Let the executions begin."

In his cell, Tab Subscript had heard the orchestra, the cheering, and the bellowing voice of his enemy Stafford on the microphone. One of the executions Stafford had spoken of was probably Subscript's, he realized with apprehension. He had spoken out against Stafford's plan to seal Eden off from the outside world. And for that he must die.

If only, he thought, hitting his puny fist against the cold steel bars, if only I had left with Danik and Dutil and the others. If only I had risked the dangers of the

105

surface — rather than remaining behind. Oh, people in the resistance thought he had stayed behind out of a sense of duty, out of the desire to rally a counter-force to Stafford. But the fact was he had stayed behind because he was afraid of what lay — out there.

*If only Danik and his men would return with the help they believed they could get on the surface.* Of course it was only a theory, a pipe dream, that Danik had. He said men walked up there, not monsters. He said that the surface people would be civilized, that he could bring some back to convince the uncon-vinced to open up Eden to the light and fresh air above. But the weeks went by and Dutil had failed to return from the surface. Then, Stafford's Civil Guard had begun rounding up all dissidents, ferreting them out of their jobs in the offices and factories of Eden, sometimes tearing their bedsheets off their cringing bodies in the middle of the night. Tyranny had come to Eden. And terror.

The large minority — about forty percent of the population — that had supported Stafford in the be-ginning had now dwindled to a few percent. But everybody was scared. Especially since the alterations at the planetarium. Once a place of rest and renewal under the artificial stars, the planetarium had become something horrible, something unknown but horrible after Stafford *altered* it. All that Subscript knew about those alterations were the results. Those per-sons arrested for violation of the new edicts would go in, and after a long while there would be screaming. And then no one would come out. No bodies, no bones — nothing.

And those new *edicts*. They were the sure sign that

Stafford was a madman.

Edict Number One—prolmugated just two weeks earlier—stated that all persons caught congregating without a permit would be subject to arrest.

Edict Number Two enlarged the small Civil Guard, previously just ceremonial soldiers stationed in front of Government Building, into a force of five thousand. This was to enforce Edict Number One.

Edict Number Three was *the elimination of Time itself*. This wasn't that impossible in Eden. For the "sun" above was stationary and constant. To remove all clocks, as Stafford ordered, effectively ended time. Stafford decided what time it was, and announced it whenever he chose to over the central PA system connected to his newly refurbished office.

Edict Number Four abolished democracy—if he hadn't done so aleady—and made Eden a kingdom.

And now Edict Number Five. The retroactive edict. All who opposed Stafford were retroactively guilty of treason.

And now the executions.

Subscript heard the heavy booted feet of the guards coming for him. He cringed, whimpered, for he was not strong and brave like Dutil. No, he would cry and scream and beg—no, no he would not.

"Your time has come to die, traitor," said the burly guard, Subscript knew that face and thick body anywhere—the head of the Civil Patrol the meanest, most dangerous man in Eden—Bdos Err. Chief of the terror. "Come with us." Subscript was savagely brought to his feet by the heavy hands of the guard and shoved out of the cell. There was no place to run, no place to hide. He determined to face his death—

probably at the scaffolds he had seen being constructed outside the Government Building shortly before he was arrested a few day earlier. Hanging — not a pleasant death.

Suprised at his own calmness he walked between the guards, head held high, toward his death. The populace stared and he heard mumbles of "must be very brave . . . damned cool traitor, isn't he . . . see how brave he is . . . " and Subscript felt proud. He would perhaps make a speech as the rope was tightened to his neck. Yes. What were those words? *Give me liberty or give me —* "

They reached the foot of the steps. He looked up at Stafford, said, "You may hang me but you have not scared me."

"Who's going to hang you, brother?" Stafford said with a wide smirk appearing on his thin lips. "Take him to the Planetarium."

"The — the — planetarium?" Subscript stuttered. "N-no, not the planetarium . . . please . . . I beg you — " His knees felt weak, they collapsed under him. The guards dragged him whimpering away.

"Not the planetarium, oh please, God, not that . . . not the planetarium."

"Let them hear the traitor cry and beg," Stafford yelled. "Let them all know that the traitors are cowards, weak men. Let them all know that the planetarium awaits all who oppose me."

Lowered eyes everywhere around the town square attested to the degree of fear that the new ruler had managed to inject into the day's activities. "Now," said Stafford, "let the hangings begin. The first hanging is of Ren Newname, for the crime of eating more than his quotient . . ."

The first of the regular criminals were brought forth, screaming and struggling, and placed upon the scaffold. Death would come to them, but only the traitors need fear the planetarium.

Bored eventually by the jerking bodies, which soon filled the six scaffolds, Stafford yawned. He said, "That will be all for today—everyone back to their jobs—and be very conscientious," and went into the building behind the throne.

With his engineers he went over the drawings of the city. He pointed to the map of the Cave of Tombs, the cave where the honored dead of Eden lay at rest. It has higher than the rest of the complex. "Finish the shaft for the surface probe here." He jabbed at the map . . . They nodded.

They trooped off to the work Stafford had assigned.

Stafford retired to his study, where he tried to watch a video tape. He soon drifted of to sleep, smiling. He was dreaming of firing the Factor Q canister up the shaft in the Hall of Tombs, forever ending the fractious demands of some Edenites to go up to the surface.

If the surface isn't totally unlivable now, he smiled, it will soon be.

# Chapter 12

Rockson and his companions had reached the approximate area of Yumak City. As a matter of fact, the sextant readings on the smeary sun low in the southwest indicated that they couldn't be more than a mile from the city of five thousand. Where the hell was it? The coordinates that Rock had been given back in Century City were the coordinates the Yumak people themselves had given Rath. Was this some kind of sick joke? Bringing the Freefighters into the middle of nowhere?

There were some scraggly bushes around. Rockson saw nothing else. "Let's take a break," Rock said, down in the dumps. "Maybe when I have some tea I can find out what is going on here."

They made a small fire with some twigs and McCaughlin brewed some tea in a bent metal pot. The dogs hunkered down to get some rest on the inch or so of snow. To them the just-above-freezing weather was a heat wave, and they liked to sleep through heat waves.

Rockson sat on a small boulder and sipped his mug of hot tea slowly. And then he heard Detroit exclaim, "Rockson, those bushes are—moving."

As Rockson looked up, the bushes were thrown aside by laughing Indians of the Yumak tribe. The tallest of the bunch of camouflage experts walked toward Rockson, hand extended.

By their odd outfits, Rockson realized that these villagers must be related to the Crazy Alligator tribe he'd spent an uncomfortable visit with years ago. The Yumak were wearing moccasins—that's how they'd sneaked up quietly. But that was about the only strictly Indian gear they wore.

The tall Indian, a hook-nosed man about seven one in height, shoot Rockson's hand. "How," he articulated, "are you?"

"Fine," Rockson answered. "I'm glad to see you—I presume you're Chief Smokestone?"

"Yes."

The man was deep tan, bare-armed, ten or twelve red feathers in a headband. He wore a rawhide tasseled jacket, and a like pair of pants. All the material was covered with beadwork of blue and red, intricate scenes of fantastic birds and animals. He had a metal breastplate that seemed to be from a twentieth-century car. A hubcap that was shined to perfection. Its barely visible insignia said OLDSMOBILE. The man's face was rugged, with deep-set dark eyes and high cheekbones. His muscled arms looked as full of sinewy strength as Rockson's.

"Where did you put your city, Smokestone? Aren't we near it?"

Smokestone laughed heartily. "You are less than a

112

hundred meters from it. Come, you will see. But first may I introduce my son and nephew. Steelring and Wild Horse."

The two braves approached and shook Rockson's hand. They too had what appeared to be polished up ancient car hubcaps tied together as breast and shoulder plates. They had no feathers. Both looked around twenty, and strong. The two braves wore their hair in two pigtails. They had pants made of some sort of multicolored cloth that shimmered like the rainbow, and were bare chested. Wild Horse wore an armband that had a little naked plastic doll of the dime-store variety tied to it.

"You have some very interesting-looking sled dogs there," Steelring said, pointing to the team that McCaughlin had driven to the spot.

"They're not sled dogs, they're sled *wolf*-dogs. And keep away from them, they bite." McCaughlin said possessively.

"Well, what is it — do you want to leave them tied here? It would be hard to get the dogs down the cliff ladders."

"Cliff ladders?"

"Yes. You see, it's the only way to get down to our city. Maybe a look would be worth a thousand words. You can tie the dogs to that cactus over there."

"Give the dogs a rest," McCaughlin said. "They can use it." Rockson agreed. "Tie them up here, we'll come back for them, — hopefully with some food — later."

"Glad to meet you all," Rockson muttered. "But we have to get some transportation from your tribe and move quickly, Smokestone. Please lead on to your—

113

invisible — city."

"This I've gotta see," said McCaughlin, packing up the pot and cups and joining Rockson and the others in their walk across the barren plain with the chief and his two young relatives.

As they walked, mystified as to where they were headed, Rockson was asked by Smokestone if he knew Trickster Deity, leader of the Crazy Alligator tribe.

"Unfortunately I do. I spent some time with him and his tribe once. I give the experience mixed reviews."

"I understand. He's my distant cousin, but he's sort of the black sheep of the family. Be careful now, walk slower all of you. Or you will fall into our beloved city."

Rockson stopped when the chief put up his hand, and so did the others. "Golly," McCaughlin said, "Will you have a look at that?"

Their feet were at the edge of a thousand-foot precipice. They were staring down into a circular hole in the ground about a hundred yards across. There were buildings, similar to Pueblo Indian cliff houses, carved into the opposite wall of the fantastic hole. And people were moving about the dwellings. Lots of people.

"We were afraid you would ride your odd-looking sleds right down into the abyss, so we three came up to greet you. Our remote-sensing devices — atop that mesa, the tall thin one about twelve miles back — tracked some electronic device you have with you."

Rockson turned to the Russian, fumed, *"That's it,* Scheransky — You're leaving that damned Schecter weather device *here* with the Yumaks."

Rona changed the subject: "Chief, did your people always live out here?"

"My ancestors were urban Indians. Los Angeles. When our vision-seekers saw the nuke war coming, they left the city, en masse, trekked to a cavern, a big one, exposed for the first time in thousands of years by the nuke quakes. Some of us stayed there. Others thought living in a big cave was spooky so we went south. And here we are. We found this swell place. It used to belong to the ancient Anasazi Indians. They built most of the place, we just improved it."

Smokestone was the first to start descending, using barely visible footholds in the rock as a ladder.

"Watch yourself now, friends," he cautioned, "be sure to place your feet in the same places I do. There's food and drink aplenty awaiting you—and some excellent motorcycles for continuing your mission."

Rock was second to begin descending. The footholds and hand niches were adequate, but he couldn't talk, he had to concentrate so carefully to make it. He wondered how the heck they got motorcycles up and down the canyon. Then he saw a rope device—some sort of elevator—far across the circular structure, near the houses. A platform of bent and shaped wood planks—more like a big basket without sides. Could that four-by-six basket on thin ropes hold a Harley?

Once they all descended, they were invited into a sandstone dwelling, and Indian maidens brought water and food. "This is wonderful," exclaimed Danik. "But we must not tarry."

Later, while the others were received by a group of

high tribal officials, the chief took Rockson on a brief tour. From the erudite quality of the conversation, it soon became evident that Smokestone was a remarkable and educated man.

His house was highest on the cliff, accessed, Rock was happy to discover, by a series of sturdy ladders. They went up.

The home of the chief was most remarkable. Like the other dwellings it was a Pueblo-style, and bare of adornment, or even of glass in the windows. There was a fireplace, with a few embers being cared for by a pretty woman. There were bookcases—hundreds of shelves. All the classics—in five languages one could read Dickens, Cooper, Disney, Heinlein, and Proust—plus thousands of technical books dating from before World War Three. Rockson also found a newly bound twelve-volume *History of the Southwestern Indians in the 20th and 21st Centuries* by Chief Smokestone. "I am not finished with it," Smokestone said, as Rockson removed one volume from the shelf and started thumbing through it.

"Quite impressive," the Doomsday Warrior said.

"I am adding a volume," said Smokestone, "so that people in the future will know of us, and of our ways. Perhaps it will help them. The air is very dry hereabouts, and the books keep well. But just in case I am having them all transferred to hard disk in our computer room."

"It seems," said Rockson, "that you have updated these ancient dwellings."

"We do what we can," Smokestone replied modestly. He showed the Doomsday Warrior more of the complex—cafeteria-style communal eating areas, gymnasiums with stone barbells, and of course the computer room—deep in the interior of the living rock. Must have been hard carting it all down here.

After seeing all their progress Rockson was more than happy to retire to the Indian chief's study and discuss their relative philosophies while the rest of the team looked around, led by eager Indian maidens, who expertly elucidated the many sights for them.

After inquiring about how Rockson's trip had been so far, and Rockson saying "Not too bad" laconically, the subject got heady. As usual among men of learning, the discussion turned to the Great Nuclear War. And the usual Monday-morning quarterbacking got more intense than usual. The Indian chief insisted that if the Indians had run the world, the war would never have happened.

"Please explain that," Rockson asked.

Smokestone had put on a softer loose shirt and lit up a pipe with a pungent tobacco. He offered Rockson some—there were many pipes—and Rockson accepted one. He puffed away too. They could, Rockson mused, be sitting in an ancient English mens' club lined with books, and not in the middle of a primitive cliff dwelling in Arizona. Smokestone, between puffs of the stuff which tasted better than it smelled to Rockson, went on with his remarks.

"When the Indian nations owned America, they respected nature, worked with it. To us, to all the tribes, the earth was our mother. To dig up huge tracts of land with giant shovels was evil. Just as you cannot dig holes in your mother's breasts with a knife—the Indian thought of the land as our mother. The land repaid us for our respect, and fed us, and

117

the cycle of life was complete.

"Neither did the the Indians—the native Americans—consider the land dividable. We couldn't own the land, instead it owned us. Our way was—and is—to walk with the beauty, to know that the spirit of land and sky and man are one whole. The white man lost that identification to the earth. They took away the soil, dug it up and refined it, made it into uranium, and then into thermonuclear bombs. To destroy themselves, and us, and the land and the air and water, in all the ten directions.

"It all started a hundred years before the war. The fences went up—barbed wire, then razor wire. The white man said to the native Americans: 'This piece is my land, and this piece is your land,' and gave themselves the better land. Then the white man discovered oil, and it was on the Indian lands. And they said, 'Wait a minute, sorry about that, *this* piece of land is not your land either, so get off.' And the Indian nations were moved again to even dryer, more remote and useless lands. And still we, the Arapaho, the Cheyenne, the Hopi, the Dineh, survived.

"Then this wasn't enough. The white man found an evil element—plutonium, the deadliest, most unnatural element of all—could be made out of a whole lot of another element—uranium. And guess where all the uranium was? Right, it was on the useless scrubland of the Indian reservations. But the times had become liberal, so they couldn't just take Indian land anymore. They would have the Indians sell it cheap to the big corporations. But the Indians would not sell their mother, the earth.

So the companies found the few Indians that

wanted to sell—Indians that had ceased to be Indians—and made them into the tribal councils. They did this by holding elections. Even though the company men knew Indians ways were different. To an Indian, *not* voting is a negative vote. Just not showing up at the polls means they vote *against* this new council. But the newspapers reported that the elections were held, and though turnout of voters was low, the Indians who wanted to sell the digging rights to our land *won* the elections.

"And so all was done legally. The earth was raped, a knife was dug into our mother's heart and the uranium dug up, to make plutonium, and the plutonium to make bombs.

"If the white men could understand that nature is a unity, if he could *walk in the beauty*, he would not disturb nature. There would not be any big holes in the mesa land, and no uranium and no bombs to destroy everyone and everything under the sun and stars."

Rockson found himself largely agreeing with the chief. Still, the Doomsday Warrior said, "Some of the uranium was used to make power plants, to supply electricity to the big cities. Not all of it was used for bombs. What was wrong with that?"

"The sun could provide as much or more power for nothing. The greed of the big companies was to make nuclear power plants, and so control all the energy, sell all the energy that people could gather free from the sun and the wind. And the nuclear power plants spread radiation death even before they were targeted by Soviet ICBMS. One plant, located in the Ukrainian slave state and run by the Russians, exploded three years before the war — in 1986. The cancer rate in Europe doubled. No, Rockson, it was as I say to you — the utility companies here in the United States, and the government fat cats in Russia, wanted nuclear power to enslave the people.

"White man — or should I say *paleface*, for some whites did understand, it wasn't a racial thing — never understood. Paleface never understood that he was a part of the cycle of nature. He didn't understand that nature is a reflection of the Great Spirit, that man is part of that great spirit, as is every rock and tree and mountain. The white man's religions all said man was separate from nature, greater than nature. Such *conceit*."

"There were some white people who believed as you do, Chief. They saw what was happening and tried to stop it."

"These people," said Smokestone, "I would call Indians. They are American Indians in spirit, though their skin is white. I believe that you, Rockson, are such a man — a white indian."

The Doomsday Warrior was touched by the compliment; he could only say, "Thank you, Chief, you do me an honor."

"To be an Indian is not a matter of race — it is a state of mind. Did you know that in the 1850s, when Indians captured white women, we took them into the tribe? And if they learned to be squaws they were welcome. The nonracist Indians did this because the long-knives — the cavalry — had depleted our numbers in the war of genocide. Indians took in runaway slaves too. We Indians were never bent on genocide, just on saving the earth — the precious land we

120

roamed. We failed to do this." Smokestone's pipe had been used up; he put it down.

"The human race failed," Rockson said, "all of us."

"You will see the seeds of the destruction, Rockson; I have assembled it all in the Hall of Atrocities — come with me. You will see how humankind defiled the Great Spirit."

# Chapter 13

After walking down a long rock-hewn corridor deep into the canyon wall, Rockson was ushered into a room the size of a good-sized ballfield. It was loaded with exhibit cases.

"Take a look at the first case on the right," Chief Smokestone said.

Rockson did. There were photographs, blown up to two by three feet—the inside of some sort of metal building—and what was inside made him nearly sick. "This is a real photograph?"

"Yes. Before the war, the Great Nuke War, the meat for American tables was raised this way—cows in small cells, confined, force-fed. The reason was greed. Cattle that don't move gain weight faster. Of course we Indians believe that animals, like man, are part of the Great Spirit. They are killed for meat, to eat. But they are respected, not tortured, Rockson. Only meat from animals roaming free, Indians believe, is healthy. These photographs are proof of the fall of man—his ignorance of the way of the Spirit."

"I had no idea," Rockson said, "that twentieth-century civilized man did such things—even the Soviet occupation forces are hardly more cruel. It takes a sadistic bent of mind to treat animals in such ways."

"There's more," said Smokestone. "Here is a small sample of the way the chickens were stacked one atop another, in thirty-story buildings with a thousand wire mesh cages one atop the other."

Rockson saw the pictures, and there was even a cutaway diorama. The birds were tightly confined, never allowed to move, unable to flex their wings or avoid the rain of excrement from above. The cages were stacked thirty, even fifty atop one another. In thousands of rows.

"And people consumed the meat of these cattle and chickens?"

"By the time of the war, ninety percent of all beef and poultry sold in the United States was raised in close confinement. The meat of these diseased, tortured animals was sold in every food market, as if there was nothing wrong. People chose not to know or they didn't care. Of course these animals' flesh had lot of residues of chemicals and antibiotics that were used to raise them quickly. Naturally, they passed on a lot of cancers and leukemias to their eaters. Aside from the cruelty of raising animals in such ways, there was that danger to the consumers.

"In the late 1980s most of the beef supply and chicken supply was made into ground patties or chunks and sold in small styrofoam coffins in places called fast-food outlets. The rusting remnants of such places still clutter the roadsides in parts of America to this day."

"The stuff couldn't have tasted very good," Rockson said.

"Correct. But to hide the bitter cardboard-like taste, the patties and chunks were injected with tons of salt and sugar. Even Indians ate such food toward the end of that decadent era. Even we, the people of the land, defied the Earth mother and ate such abominations. Of course, most Indians had lost their treaty rights to hunt and fish by that time, so what choice did they have but to go to these places too?

"The paleface civilization didn't understand consequences would result *kharmically* from its treatment of animals. Millions more animals were needlessly tortured in research in laboratories, often for the most frivolous reasons. Here, come with me to the next exhibit — see? It is a lab with cats with electrodes attached to their brains — and this exhibit. Here the dogs have their heads severed and attached to feeder tubes."

Rockson could hardly look at the exhibits. He moved on. There was a huge photograph — black and white, of a beautiful Arizona mesa jutting from the morning mists.

"That photo," Smokestone said, "was taken in the 1930s — of Black Mesa."

"A beautiful area. Untouched."

"Therein dwelled the earth spirits. The world is balanced at four places, Rockson. Of course you know that. One of these places is called the first corner. Black Mesa sat upon this sacred balancing place. On the map of the U.S. it was, ironically, the place where four states — Colorado, Arizona, New

125

Mexico, and Utah—touched.

"Now look at the next photo—a color photograph taken from the air—taken of the same area in 1989—just before World War Three.

Rockson whistled. There were giant smokestacks and part of the mesa was gone. The mesa had been eaten away as if by a giant. No—there were the instruments of its destruction—skyscraper-tall steam shovels. It was obvious from their lineup heading toward the huge power plants that they were feeding the mesa bit by bit to fuel the power plants' many furnaces. The smoke pouring out of the stacks was black and deadly.

"See those hundreds of threads on those silver poles—all heading to the west?"

"Yes. What are they?"

"Power lines—heading toward California. California virtually ate electricity, mostly for wasteful purposes. The Indian lands were cunningly seized by the lawyers of the big utilities and sacrificed to the white man's god—Sacrificed to *Mammon. Greed.*"

"And the world lost one balancing point."

"The next pictures show the result of that imbalance . . ."

Rockson walked on, his bootheels echoing down the stone floor. The next pictures were war photos. Bodies, mushroom clouds. Ruins. One picture was from a space satellite. A water-filled crater on a coastal plain.

"New York?"

"Chicago. That's Lake Michigan, Rockson."

Rockson sighed. "If only it could be undone. And yet the world is threatened again, this very day, by one man's madness."

Rockson spent some time explaining their urgent mission and the danger that Stafford presented.

"Rockson," Smokestone held his arm at the bicep, "please take me with you to this Eden. I want to be in on stopping Stafford from laying waste to the world. I want to succeed where my ancestors failed. I want to help to create the new balance. Please let me come with you."

Rockson had already gauged the man to be a worthwhile companion should he choose to come along. "You may come with us."

The Doomsday Warrior thanked the Indians for their hospitality and said the Freefighters and Danik must be off, for their mission was of utmost urgency. Smokestone had made arrangements for the dogs and sleds. He had specially souped-up old Harley 900 motorcycles assembled near the "elevator."

They rode up the elevators with the Harleys in shifts. One at a time. The elevator was sturdier than it looked, but it creaked.

Rockson had decided to keep one dog with them. They were superb sniffers—and Rockson swore he could teach Class Act, his lead dog, to be quiet.

"Especially after the dogs saved our asses from those damned voracious gophers. I think it would be a good idea to bring Class Act. She can run like hell—I'm sure she can keep up with our dirt bikes. If not, she can drop behind and catch up when we stop for rest.

So it was that they started up the big motorcycles

with a tremendous roar at the rim of the inhabited canyon. The Indians below filled the Arizona air with wild whoops and yips as the bold chief and the Freefighters set off for Eden.

Rockson really opened up his big Harley; the engine sang out a song of power, cutting the desert air, slashing over the inch-deep snow like a dream of speed and energy.

Smokestone, waving his huge stone-head tomahawk over his head, steering with one hand, pulled alongside at 135 mph, daring Rock to go faster.

The race was on, leaving the others behind in the dust and thrown snow. 160, 170, 175 mph. Rockson had handled cycles like this before; he was sure he could surpass the chief. But the Indian just kept a-comin', kept up, then sailed past, screaming out taunts and waving that tomahawk. Still with one hand — ye gods, Rock thought, I'm just an amateur compared to this ballsy guy.

Leaning down hard, Rock was determined to catch the chief, at least for a brief instant.

180,185, 190, 195 . . . . The cacti flew by, the bike shuddered and quivered up to 200 mph. He was alongside the chief.

"Yip, yip, yahooooo," Smokestone bellowed into the wind. "You are something, Rockson, really something." He slowed down, as this couldn't go on without them being eroded pieces of flesh spread across the desert — and they had a job to do. 195, 190, 185 — soon they were cruising at a mere 175.

After another ten minutes, they stopped for a sip of water from the bikes' canteens. Let the others catch up. The Indian looked Rock in the eyes and said, "I want us to be blood brothers." Rock nodded, and they made slits in their forearms and brought them together; joined forever.

# Chapter 14

The Freefighters rode their advanced-tech Harleys in V-formation across the flat desert. The motors, loud and strong, carried them as if they were on a magic carpet, quintupling the fastest speed they'd ever attained on the sleds. Danik was managing his big cycle fairly well, but couldn't keep up. He was back a ways. Danik had a sidecar, with Class Act in it.

The sheer power at Rockson's disposal made him feel restored. Having Smokestone with him was a reassurance, somehow, that the mission would succeed. The dull orange globe of the sun shone through a cloud scudded afternoon sky. It was good to be alive today.

At 3:30 P.M. they reached the old U.S.–Mexican border. Rockson and his friends stopped their bikes and waited for Danik. Danik's bike was soon on the horizon. And snuggled down in the sidecar was Class Act, howling away and "eating" the wind as he traveled. They did not wait long, as Danik was getting less and less afraid of going fast with every mile they

131

traveled. In a short while they heard his engine, and then he pulled up. The thin albino Edenite had a candy-eating grin on his face. He pulled off his helmet and said, "Eden was never like this." Class Act leapt from her perch in the sidecar and rushed to Rockson. "Good girl," Rock said, rubbing her ears and petting her. The giant red tongue licked at his face.

They took a break. The dog alongside him, panting happily, Rockson sat on his haunches looking at the shallow, fifty-foot-wide stream that was the winter version of the Rio Grande River coursing by idly. Not ten yards from his position was some rusty pipe stubs in the ground. The border fence of a century ago. If you looked carefully, the ground was discolored a bit — to the color of ocher. It was the red dust of all the barbed wire gone to corrosion. Rockson thought about how it must have been a century past: the wetbacks, struggling dirt farmers, peons by the millions trying to get across that border to join their wealthy neighbors to the north. How desperate they had been to get into the United States. How they'd envied the U.S. citizens — until the thousand flashes brighter than the sun glowed in the northern sky — until the nukes fell. Then they hadn't envied their northern neighbors anymore.

As a matter of fact, in the first few days after the blasts, new fences had been erected on the *Mexican* side of the border for a change. Wave after wave of starving diseased radiation victims poured *south*, desperate to get into Mexico.

Of course, those that had constructed Eden had done so before the nuke war, and therefore most of the Edenites were already in the vast underground biosphere when N-Day came. All except a handful. And that handful included the brains and pocketbook behind the whole project—Edward Renquist. He had not made it.

Perhaps Renquist had died in the first flashes of atomic hellfire. Danik had told that Renquist was in Austin, Texas, at the fatal hour, trying to effect a reconciliation with his wife, Sandra. Rockson saw other pathetic reminders of that day—there were white things—torn and rotted human bones—amidst all that rust on the ground. Perhaps Renquist had survived the blasts, made it to this border, and like thousands, millions of other Americans had been shot down by the Mexican Border Police, or been killed in the crush of bodies. God what a horror it must have been right on this tranquil spot!

And the Mexicans had succumbed too, by the millions—they could keep the desperate masses streaming south from crossing over, but they *couldn't* keep the radiation clouds in the north. And Mexico, too, became a haunted corpse of a country. Even though she had nothing to do with the great psychotic contest between the Eastern and Western blocs of nations, Mexico too suffered the results of that culminating madness-of-all-madness that is *nuclear war* . . .

Class Act seemed anxious to go on. She stood up and rushed back and forth on the dusty surface. Rockson petted her, pulled her ears. The tongue slipped out and ran over his wrist. "Nice wolf-doggie, nice." He turned to the group, who were already putting on their black helmets and heading to start their bikes.

"Class Act has the right idea. Let's get traveling. Prepare to cross the shallows," Rockson ordered, struggling from his reverie. "But I'll go first — with Detroit. We'll cross at that lazy bend — it's just inches deep, I hope . . . I don't want all of us to be out there together at the same time, that's too vulnerable. I don't expect any danger, but just because it looks okay, doesn't mean it is."

There was a sandy but firm bottom under the half foot of the gently moving warmish water, and so there was no need to improvise a way of keeping their vehicles dry. They easily waded their cycles across. First Rockson went across, then Detroit crossed the twenty yards of shallow water, steering his cycle with his meaty hands. Rockson and Detroit took up position in a scrubby copse of trees on the other side before the Doomsday Warrior waved the rest of the party onward.

They were in Mexico. The terrain was prairie-like, the vegetation consisting mostly of sagebrush and scattered cacti.

The motorcycles were again showing their stuff, and the group were making a good 150 miles per hour. Danik was now keeping up, and, though he had nearly failed his trial spins at Yumak City, was no longer a bit afraid.

"There wasn't much need for speed in Eden," he had explained. "The whole city-world is ten miles long by a mile wide." They slowed down. It was getting a bit muddy. There wasn't a bit of snow on the ground anymore, and a gentle rain was beginning.

They saw a purplish mountain range. Six bumps on

134

the horizon. "That's it—I remember now," Danik shouted. The tallest one—*that's where I came from.*"

Rockson urged them onward. It was nearly nightfall, the purplish sky melding with blackness to the east that was already filled with stars. The atmosphere had been thinner ever since N-Day, so even before the sun was set, you could see many of the brighter constellations.

The mountains loomed larger and larger, the terrain grew rocky, and they lost time. The last rays of sun flickered over the worn-down peaks of brown sandstone. They were more barren hills than full-fledged mountains. Rockson ordered headlamps on. They roared toward the central peak—Mt. Obispo. When the way got precipitous, Rockson raised a hand.

They stopped, and in the light of the headlamp of his big Harley, which stood up leaning on its kickstand on the gravelly surface, Rockson took out the map.

Danik concurred with Rock's assessment of their position. "We are upon the entranceway to Eden." He looked nervous, and stated, "I hadn't—I hadn't *realized* we were so close. We *must* pull back for a time. I must *explain* something to you."

"Are we at Eden City? If we are, let's get into your tunnel. We have a date with this madman Stafford."

"*No,*" Danik insisted. He was silhouetted in the light of the headlamps, looking impossibly tall and wraithlike. He said, "We must not advance to the entranceway until I *explain*—please, let us retreat behind that hill at least, until I *explain.*"

Rockson begrudgingly agreed. They turned their

135

cycles around and retreated behind the hill. Rock got quickly off his vehicle and put the kickstand down. "Now, why the hell can't we go in? Time is passing, every second counts—"

"I regret to say," admitted the Eden City citizen, "that I omitted some detail about Eden when I spoke of it. There is a danger—a real danger—in that tunnel. I said it is an old construction tunnel that no one uses—but the reason is not fear of it collapsing. There is a more fearsome reason. There are *two* parts to Eden. The tunnel, the only way in, skirts along a second underground settlement. It is called Death City. It is called that because to be near it causes death. We were faced with execution, so my party took the chance and went through that tunnel, and we made it by the skin of our teeth. There are patrols of—the Cultists."

"What *exactly* is this Death City?"

Danik sighed. "About twenty-five years after Eden was sealed off, there was a secession of a sort by a thousand followers of a sect of people that worshipped Renquist."

"*Worshipped* Renquist? The millionaire who set up the city?"

"Exactly, Rockson. Renquist had assumed the dimension of a god to those who attributed their safety to his forethought and planning, to his choosing them to survive when the world was plunged into nuclear war. Naturally, the other inhabitants thought this group a bit odd, but they were tolerated. The sect grew as troubles beset Eden—and when the women of our world became barren, after the thirtieth year of being sealed off, then the cult really grew. They

136

demanded the worship of giant statues they erected of Renquist. They said we should sacrifice a human being to the statue, so that Renquist would forgive us and all would be well again. The government refused.

"The Cultists said we would all die if we didn't worship the correct god — Renquist. They went off on their own — further into the natural caverns. This mountain is much like the Carlsbad Caverns of Virginia, which I saw pictures of in Century City. The mountain is honeycombed with giant chambers. The Renquist cultists sealed off their cavern and have seldom been *seen* since. But there were incidents of our women being carried off if they came too close to the Death City side of Eden. Women — our women — used to go to the area of the 'fresh winds,' near the waters of Eden, to drown their deformed babies. These hideous creatures started to be born shortly before the women of Eden became entirely barren.

"The babies were spirited away almost instantly. We know that because some of the women changed their minds and returned to the area to find the hideous children gone. Sometimes the *women* did not return, either. There were screams, the women's clothes were found. No amount of searching ever turned them up. We believe that they were sacrificed to the statues of Renquist in Death City."

"Why didn't you tell me that before?"

"The memories were — vague. And then as I remembered about Death City, I was afraid you would abandon the journey. For there are thousands of these fearsome Cultists. They are even more dangerous than Stafford. The cultists know of the passageway to Eden. We were in the tunnel, and we heard marching feet — we froze in position, but weird greenish lights played over us — possibly some sort of detector ray — and then gas came rolling at us. We ran — we were but a short distance from the surface — I could see the blue afternoon sky. We were — lucky . . . I am not brave. I am not a warrior. I am sorry —"

Rockson said, "Men, we must immediately post a guard . . ."

The bald stocky man with the muttonchop moustache peered over the rocks. His name was Manion. He gazed with interest at the group of strangers. One of them appeared to be an Anasazi Indian — Indians had been seen before on these patrols on the surface. But the others, dressed in military khaki, they were unusual. Wait — one of them was a woman. Manion watched the tall woman excitedly. A surface woman. A necessity for breeding purposes. And there was something about — The woman sat down and started going through a pack of supplies. She took off her big insulating jacket and the black helmet. She shook loose her long red hair. That aquiline nose, those high cheekbones — the hair — she looked like . . . It *was the Goddess Sandra*. It was. Manion had seen her photos a thousand times in the Temple, memorized her every nuance, her every gainly move, on the videotapes. He had seen the Sandra, and the God Edward Renquist to whom she was consort, strolling the streets of Dallas, Texas, in those most sacred videotapes. Yes, Manion was sure it was her. The Sandra. She had returned.

Excitedly the blue-robed figure that was Manion scurried back down the defile and told his comrades of the discovery. In whispered excitement he told them his decision. He decided that the sleep gas had to be used—the Goddess was among an odd group—perhaps she had been intercepted on her way back to the Faithful Ones of Death City. Perhaps the Sandra was a captive. Or perhaps they were merely her earthly companions, demigods appearing to be humans. "Nevertheless," Manion said, "we can't go wrong to use the gas. And we must hurry before the breeze shifts—if their vicious-looking mastiff gets our scent, we will be consumed surely."

Each of the shaved-headed followers—ten in all—loaded their silvery tube weapons with something like bazooka shells, only made of transparent plastic. The liquid inside the shells had been originally developed to handle the rioters in the late 1980s. It was still effective, though a century old. The great Renquist had stockpiled these weapons and many others knowing in his mind that the day would come when they must be used by the Devout to protect the Faith.

"Quickly, up to the top," the muttonchopped bald man said to his minions. "Fire in a circle around the intruders. Make sure you do not hit our Goddess. Anyone who harms the Sandra will be added to the Snake Temple's Mound." With that admonition the flock stealthily crawled up to the edge of the ridge and, on signal from Manion, fired their silent weapons. The gas shells exploded in a perfect circle around those below, and even their strange animals succumbed instantly.

# Chapter 15

When Rock and the others awoke it wasn't long until they realized that the one person missing was Rona Wallender.

Detroit Green ran over and lifted Danik, who was only up on one elbow, off the ground. "You skinny weird bastard," Detroit threatened, pulling back his left hand in a fist. "Your lies have resulted in Rona being taken. How do we know you aren't one of these Cultists yourself? I know you had something to do with this—you led us into a trap."

"No, no, I swear . . ." Danik stuttered. "I didn't."

"Sure you did. You already admitted not telling us about Death City—now your friends have taken away Rona—you set this up—and you're gonna admit it. Spill it—where'd they take Rona?"

Chen stayed Detroit's fist the second it started traveling for the albino's nose. "Stop, Detroit. He doesn't know—he didn't set us up . . ."

"How the hell do you know that? He lied to us—he admitted it." Detroit didn't let go of Danik's collar.

Rockson was the only one taking effective action.

141

He had crawled up on the rise and peered over to the mountain. He pulled up his electron binoculars—equipped with a night-vision mode—and scanned the area. There was no sign of the woman he cared so much for. He looked for tracks. The ground was rocky, and there were none. He scrambled back down to the arguing Freefighters and Danik.

He passed a burst-open metal thing—one of the sleep-gas shells, half buried in the soil. He touched it. A strange canister—soft metal.

As Rockson approached the noisy Freefighters, he heard the gist of the argument, which was continuing. Then he saw the position of the three—Chen holding Detroit's arm, Detroit threatening Danik, having lifted the poor man off the ground by his coat collar. Chen was saying, "Detroit, your reasoning isn't logical. If Danik did set us up, why did he warn us about the Cultists, why did he tell us to be on guard just before the attack came? We were about to take precautions. Why was only Rona taken, why are we still alive? Why is Danik still here with us?"

"I don't know the answers, Chen, but I'll bet I can beat some answers out of—"

Rockson intervened. "Chen's right, Detroit. Let Danik go. We have to find Rona. There's no sign of her. Danik," snapped the Doomsday Warrior, "where's the entrance to the tunnel. We're going in after her."

Danik said, "I—I think I can find it. Just over the hill near the three big boulders." Then he added most pathetically, "I didn't plan this—I'm sorry. It's all my— It is all my fault—please forgive me . . . I will do what I can to help you free her before she is

142

sacrificed . . . ."

"Never mind that," said Rockson. "Find me that hole in the ground, Danik. If we run into them, and the Cultists object to releasing her immediately . . ." Rockson unholstered his shotpistol and raised it, "this will take care of them."

The team was all together on this sentiment. It was time for manly action. Archer growled and lifted his steel crossbow over his head, Chen *wooshed* his nunchaku sticks, McCaughlin lifted his Liberator rifle, joining in the tumult of anger.

Within minutes, the Edenite had led them through a bizarre jumble of oddly shaped rocks, looking for strange symbols that were drawn on certain stones. He found them. They paused at the tunnel entrance. It was wide enough for one man at a time to squeeze through. Class Act, sniffing madly, on the scent from the hat Rockson had let her smell — Rona's hat — led them on eagerly.

Rockson, then McCaughlin, squeezed through; they helped the others drop down the six feet to the floor of the tunnel. It was Scheransky's turn. "I feel like we're going down the rabbit hole — and I'm no Alice," said Scheransky.

"Never mind the allusions to literature, get down here," Rock said, pulled on the Russian's dangling legs. McCaughlin had his flashlight on, so they could see.

One by one they cautiously dropped into the hole, lighting their torches when they hit the floor. Archer and McCaughlin had to crouch to stand inside. Slowly they advanced down the narrow passageway hewn from the living rock of Mt. Obispo.

Rockson let the mutant canine go ahead of them. There were twists and turns in the tunnel Danik admitted that he didn't remember, and forking passages. He did his best to keep them on the right track, but in a matter of ten minutes, despite his best efforts, they were lost in the maze. Rockson had been dropping little torn pieces of notebook paper behind them, in case they had to retrace their steps. He said there was no danger of being lost, and all should push on. It was growing warmer, and they opened their combat parkas and loosened their shirt collars. "Archer," Rock whispered, "stop clanking your crossbow against the damned walls."

"Meee tight—"

"Shhh," Rockson implored. "Class Act has frozen in place—there is something ahead."

Sure enough, in a short time the dog's instincts had proved correct. Shuffling noises, mutters of male voices. "Douse the lights." But Rock had them turned on again when he realized there were no lights ahead in the direction of the noises. The floor vibrated; they were very close to the enemy. Rock was the first to figure it out. "We're not in the right tunnel, but this tunnel is right next to the correct one—feel along the walls, everybody. Find out where the vibration is coming from."

By the time the marching feet faded, they had decided that the footfalls and voices were to the right of their slow descent. The Freefighter team started digging with the sharp ends of their metal batons. The walls were porous rock here, and came out in chunks. "Keep the hole just wide enough to crawl through," Rock admonished.

It took two hours to go the six feet and reach the other tunnel. First just a little hole showed light, then, cautiously, they widened their opening. Rock crawled through to find himself up on a ledge above another tunnel, a bigger one. There was a dull flickering light and some footfalls far off. The others were advised to slip through. They packed along the shelf of rock, nearly turning over some small barrels and boxes.

"Death City," gasped Danik. "Now that we are here, it's six of us and the dog against a thousand fanatical Cultists."

"Let me worry about that—you just keep up with us."

"Yeah, and keep *quiet*," McCaughlin added.

They huddled down as soldiers—or at least what looked like soldiers—bald tall men in blue uniforms bearing long silver tubes on their shoulder straps—passed underneath them.

"We need some of those uniforms," Rockson said. "We don't have a prayer of rescuing Rona unless we get some disguises."

They watched the ten soldiers, who seemed to patrol this part of the tunnel, pass underneath the rock shelf six times, and the Doomsday Warrior timed their movements.

There was only once course of action—attack the ten men, silently, without use of the rifles or shotpistols.

On Rockson's approval, Chen handed to both Danik and Scheransky one *shuriken*. Only Chen and Rockson were proficient in throwing the lethal little five-bladed knives, but they might get lucky.

145

Rock and Chen poised their own star-knives. "Aim for their Adam's apples. If we get more than two, that will help. Archer—you use your arrows. Hit them someplace that will avoid their crying out. You too, Danik. Then we jump the ones still standing—before they can call out. I hope this works. Try not to make it too bloody either—we have to use those uniforms."

"I'll throw, but whether I hit one or not, I'll jump down and use my cudgel," said Scheransky.

Archer silently lifted his bow into the air and smiled. "I will doooo twoooo," he growled.

"You really think you can skewer two at a time?"

Archer nodded up and down vigorously, and removed the longest barbed arrow Rock had ever seen from his quiver and set it in the steel crossbow's slot.

"We're counting on *everyone* scoring."

Danik whispered, "But I never killed—"

"This will be your first time then, Danik," Rock said, and winked. "You can do it."

They waited till the right moment. Right after the guards had passed, they let fly with the star-knives. Rockson's and Chen's made target, bringing their men down gurgling out blood. Scarcely a noise passed their lips. The Russian's swooshing blade hit his man in the temple and that shut him up. He didn't even flop around, just fell dead.

Archer's huge arrow flew with a hiss and went right through the neck of the next man in line and out his throat, and, remarkably, right back into the man in front of him. Skewered together, gasping out quarts of blood, they tumbled to the side, their eyes wide and staring at darkness.

The Freefighters were upon the remaining Cult soldiers before they had a chance to whirl around. Scheransky bludgeoned down his prey with ease, cracking open the man's skull and spilling his brains on the stone floor. Detroit slammed his baton into the base of his man's skull. Scratch one more Cultist. Smokestone's massive tomahawk spilled brains right and left.

Rockson smashed the last man a mighty blow to the solar plexus with his balisong knife handle as the soldier was already raising the long silver tube and squeezing the trigger on the thing. Rockson winced, expecting a shot, even though the tube wasn't pointed at him — and never would be. But instead of a report, the tip of the silver tube glowed red. A section of the wall it was facing started smoking and glowing red-hot. The man stopped pulling the trigger when his eyes rolled up and he fell.

They had managed to get them all without making more than some scuffling noises, a few gurgles, and death rattles. "Now, quickly, put on their uniforms — let Archer and McCaughlin use the outfits of those two big guys, the rest catch-as-catch-can."

# Chapter 16

*Meanwhile, deep in the earth* . . . a strange torchlit procession descended. Six pale loin-clothed figures carried a sedan chair on their massive shoulders. In front of the figures was the short swarthy man with the characteristic muttonchop beard and moustache that designated him as a Renquist high priest. Manion had switched from his coarse outer-world garment, and now he wore a heavily ornate blue silk robe. Those carrying his captive on the sedan chair behind him were the servants of his exalted being. Behind the bearers of the ornate sedan chair were the six soldier-monks who had so accurately fired the sleep gas.

They have done well, they will be rewarded, Manion thought. The *Sandra* has been acquired, the destiny of the people of Death City, and her exalted destiny was about to be fulfilled. Renquist, Mightiest of All will have his Queen once more. And the Blessed Renquist will reward his people. Manion, when he first had peeked over the rocks of the outside world and had seen the Goddess and her companions, had known at once. The Goddess was exactly as she eternally appeared—beautiful, red flames for hair, tan of complexion, long of limb. Haughty, and buxom. She *was* the Sandra, consort-wife of the Renquist. She had been sent back to them, so that destiny could at last be fulfilled. Manion had no doubt of that. She was Sandra. And she belonged to his people.

But what of the others with her—those strange men? Couldn't they have been messengers that heaven sent to deliver Sandra to Death City. No, they must have been a group of surface people that had seized the Goddess, and were about to take her for their own. Manion was not entirely sure, so he had thought it best to not kill them where they lay overcome with the gas of sleep. They would awaken and they would be afraid and leave the area. Yes. They would not try to follow—and even if they found the entrance, there were patrols in the tunnels. Still, he was uneasy. Perhaps he should have killed them . . .

The entourage bearing the sleeping woman reached a cavern, and a huge brass door with carved figures of a titanic bear stood before them. Manion, as was his duty, went to the gong and took up the stick and rang it twice. Responding to the sonorous ringing, the doors slowly opened.

In the flickering flame-lamp's light, twenty meters beyond the door, stood the ten-story-high solid gold statue of Renquist. Manion made a prostration, and then those behind him set down the sedan chair and also made obeisance, their foreheads to the stone floor below them. The Fire of Eternity set before the huge statue flared up. "A good sign," Manion interpreted aloud. "Renquist is well pleased."

The Goddess was paraded before the statue, the gossamer covering of the sedan chair removed so that *He* could see. Then Manion ordered that the Goddess be taken to her new quarters, to be bathed in milk and honey, to be dressed properly, so that all might be fulfilled . . .

Rona regained consciousness shortly after being deposited on a vermilion silk bed. The awakening was soft, and slow. Rona had dim memories of a sweet dream, of beautiful milkmaids combing out her long tresses, bathing her, caressing her, stripping her of dirty garments and bathing her in milk. Suddenly, she sat bolt upright. Where was she—what had happened? She started to rise, and felt her body, shorn of her khaki outfit, nearly naked, slide across the silk. She gasped when she saw that all she wore was a scanty, jewel-encrusted brassiere and a stingy bikini bottom. The flimsiest gossamer transparent skirt hung from that bottom, hiding nothing of her long legs.

She saw an ornate gold-framed mirror in the corner of the large empty room. No doors or windows visible. This must be a dream. She went to the mirror. There she was, her hair neat and clean, in the bare-midriff costume. There was a ruby-encrusted tiara on her head. She took it off. She felt along the walls for a door. Nothing. Had the milkmaids been real? Was this real? She looked around. There was the dresser and mirror, the brocaded silk sofa-bed, a carpet that belonged in an antique store — a sumptuously appointed Louis XIV type room. It was subtly lit by recessed bulbs in its rock ceiling.

There were giggles. Watchers in the walls — somewhere. She went to the bed and tore off the bedspread, covered her scantily clad body. She stood there, for a long time, almost breathless. Nothing. Rona lay back down again and closed her eyes. The bed sure felt real enough. She touched the jewels on her bikini button. Hard. Real. She moved her hand to her perfumed left nipple, which, due to the briefness of the brassiere, was half exposed, and squeezed. "Ouch," she exclaimed aloud, "This is real. Where the hell am I?"

No answer. Then, from the dark corners of the room, squat, heavily veiled figures crept forward silently. Rona gasped, stood up on her bare perfumed feet, and took a karate stand, hands made into cutting, crushing instruments of death. "Who's there?"

Giggles. One figure came forward a bit further, into the light. It was a short wide woman of about thirty years of age, hairless, and dressed in a set of coarse shapeless veils of a light blue cotton-type material from neck to ankles. "I am Verna, Your Majesty," the woman said, and bowed deeply.

"Where am I?" Rona said. She did not change her *kata* position. "What is this place? Who dressed me — undressed me —"

"We, your handmaidens prepared you, Your Majesty."

"Prepared me for *what*?"

"You are to achieve your destiny, oh Sandra,

152

Mother of All."

"Huh?"

Rona whirled as the hidden door opened again. In stepped a bald man in muttonchop beard and moustache. He looked much like those nineteenth-century portraits of the scions of American capitalism — except that below his face he wore not a pin-striped suit but a blue bejeweled tunic of some sort. Kind of a Roman outfit.

He too bowed deeply. Rona thought, At least I get some respect around here, wherever here was. "What's going on?" she demanded. "Where am I and who are you?"

"Your obedient servant, Jefferson Manion, at your service," the man said. "Sandra Renquist, Your Exalted Goddess, Your Supreme Majesty, you are in Death City, your people have brought you here. So that you may be joined with He Who Is Eternal."

He bowed again.

"I'm going to kick you in your stupid face unless you—"

The man raised a small stick he carried and a flickering ray jumped from it into the mid-forehead of the captive. She paused in mid-sentence, and a beatific smile errupted upon her face. Rona felt good—very good. She couldn't remember what she had been angry about. All these people were so nice and respectful. Did it *really* matter where she was?

"That's much better," Manion said, lowering his weapon of delights. "You will remember soon, Your Majesty. "We will teach you what you must have forgotton on the awesome journey down here from the heavens above. All will be as it has been written."

153

The high priest Manion led bemused and scantily clad Rona down the corridors outside her sumptuous room toward the great metal door with the bear emblazoned upon it—he led her to the Temple of Renquist, the holiest place in Death City.

Once inside, amid the thousands of candles and before the enormous statue that was of a man in a suit, a man with a gold muttonchop beard and moustache, Manion said to Rona, "He wants you, and he will have you."

Rona was unsteady on her feet, her elbows supported by two handmaidens. However, her mind was clearing from its pleasant indecisive state. And she was putting two and two together. The gas she'd seen erupting from a popping shell. An attack. Then awakening in the strange room—the nonsense about her being Sandra.

She had been kidnapped by the Death City Cultists. They thought she was this Sandra, somebody they worshipped. They were planning something for her—possibly a sacrifice to their damned god, the Renquist. Well, that would not happen.

Quickly the near-naked Freefighter gauged the situation. Manion, the handmaidens—pushovers. But in the flickering light of the candles—a dozen or more helmeted guards, all with guns of some sort holstered at their waists. Not good. Play along for a while, find out what gives here.

"Please tell me—the things I must do," she said, still playing bemused, complacent Sandra. "Please tell me so that I might do the right thing and please the Renquist."

Manion smiled. "That's better, much better—I was

worried for a while that you, despite your appearance, might not be the Sandra, the One for Renquist."

"What would happen were I not the Sandra?"

"Immediate torture-execution for defiling the sacred Temple. Your bones would join the bejeweled skulls and femurs that make up the punishment mound in the Sanctuary of the Snake."

"I *am* the Sandra," Rona said with utter conviction in her voice.

"Then, I will show you what is to be for you. What your sacred duty will be after the remarriage."

"Lead on, oh priest Manion," Rona said. *Remarriage?* What's that about, Rona wondered, as they left the temple by a small side door and plunged into a steeply slanting tunnel that grew increasingly cold. She noticed footsteps. The dozen soldiers had fallen in behind their small party. *Damn.*

It became even colder; they threw a smock over her. The handmaidens each placed a bejeweled slipper upon each cold foot.

"These are ice caves," she observed, looking around at the giant color-bright ice stalagmites on both sides of their route. What happens here?"

"Here is preserved the blessed seed of the Renquist. For use after your marriage ceremony."

"Seed?"

"Yes, the frozen semen of our Founder-God Renquist. You will again be his wife, his Goddess Queen. And you will be impregnated with his seed. The Renquist stored his seed here—in the ice. He called it, 'Eden Sperm Bank.' You will bear his child to become our prince. Though the Renquist has left his human body these past hundred and five years, yet he will bear us a leader—through you, Sandra."

"What a privilege," Rona muttered. The guards, or whatever they were, were double the original number now, and she was deeper into this damned cold place. This was worse than the time she'd been kidnapped by the Nazis and they'd mistaken her for Eva Braun, Hitler's mistress. The Nazis at least hadn't expect her to bear a dead man's child.

But being tortured to death seemed the only alternative. At the moment.

# Chapter 17

Rona had to do something, *anything*. So what she did was, at a section of the slanting cold corridor that bent and narrowed, stumble. It was not a real stumble; Rona was catlike on her feet. It was a pretended stumble, to lurch her closer to one of the soldier-monks. She let his hands come up from his holstered long silver weapon, then she made a grab for it. The damned gun, or whatever it was, was so long—about two feet—that she hadn't cleared the holster with it before the iron grip of Manion's hands stayed her move. Then she was hit across the face by the guard who she had lunged at, a glancing fist to the jaw that made her see stars. She was wrestled to the ground by the two handmaidens, who were stronger than they looked.

Cursing a blue streak, the hellcat Freefighter did her best with the mob of restrainers, but she felt her hands being drawn behind her back and being lashed securely together with some sort of smooth strong rope.

"Now," said Manion, gasping for breath as he lifted Rona to her feet, "We will proceed. I do not understand this behavior, but I hope you are not injured. Why did you do this?"

Her answer was full of ripe Freefighter expletives; she kicked out and struggled like a banshee. Then Manion lifted his red flickering trank-stick, and aimed it at her. The broadest smile of benevolence she'd ever worn came across Rona's angry flushed face. She forgot what the tumult was about. Rona complacently moved along, happy suddenly to be in the company of such fine folks.

They went through an open set of bronze doors into a darkened chamber. Torches hung on the wall lit the scene of macabre elegance—chairs of carved stone, elaborate wall decorations of large snakes, intertwined. As a matter of fact, the whole chamber was snake-motif.

And dimly, in the smoky incense-filled far end of the rectangular high-ceilinged rock chamber, stood the full-length standing statue of the Renquist. The statue was of stone, a pale pink marble several stories high. The statue was dressed in a size-300 cloth pinstripe suit—as if it were a real person, to be well dressed for a board meeting. Several bald men were bowing and scraping in front of the statue, at some sort of hump. As they approached the hump, Rona saw that it was a mound of irregular shape, some four feet high. It was composed of cemented-together, jewel-encrusted bones. Human bones. How nice, she thought, in her dreamlike state of bliss.

They led her around the hump, and the maroon-robed keepers of the chamber took her, one by each elbow, without struggle, to the statue of a snake, a six-foot-tall standing cobra of black onyx. The snake's mouth was wide open, and was hissing out some sort of icy breath. There was a rod in the mouth of the snake, all covered with ice, buried in the length of the snake's body with just the end sticking out, like a forked snake-tongue.

"Behold," said Manion. "The sperm bank, the seed of the Renquist, preserved for one hundred and six years for this blessed moment."

They removed her coverings, so that she stood shivering in her gossamer and scant bikini and bra, to the right side of the stone snake. Manion went over and bowed before the immense Renquist statue, and took up a book — a Bible — and headed back solemnly to stand before Rona, who was drawn by the monks to stand beside the stone snake. Manion opened the Bible and lifted his hands in a genuflecting gesture that made the sign of the star. He intoned, "Who gives the bride?"

And he answered himself, "I do."

"Do you, Sandra the Renquist, again take as your lord and master and husband this God, the sacred Edward Renquist, as your lawful and divine husband, till the end of time?"

Rona said, "Wha?"

"Say yes," Manion whispered in exasperation.

Rona was woozy; she thought she was in Century City's chapel with Rockson, all six foot two of his manly presence, standing next to her. She was getting married. Good. It was about time.

"Yes, I do," She said firmly.

Manion smiled, "Then by the power invested in me

as chief priest of the Sacred Holiest of Holies, I pronounce you God and Goddess—proceed with the chastisement and impregnation." He slammed shut the Bible and tossed it to one of the monks, who caught it and placed it back near the statue.

They led her away, through the near darkness, with strains of organ music played on the stalactites echoing eerily around her. "Hey, doesn't Rock get to walk with me? Where the rice?"

She was coming out of it. Why were her hands tied behind her back? "Say, what kind of a wedding is this, anyway—who—"

She started struggling, wriggling. She was held firmly by her elbows. This time by powerful soldier-monk's hands.

They took her to the mound. The mound was about six feet in diameter and curved up to a maximum of three feet off the floor in the center. It was made of semiprecious stones—agates, turquoise, coral—all cut into one-inch-square mosaic tiles. Rona could see the depiction of a coiled cobra snake on it. It took six of them to bend her over, stomach down, on the mound. They untied her wrists, only to retie them to some rings set at the edge of the mound. They likewise, spreading her powerful legs wide, affixed her ankles to some golden rings set in the floor. She found herself spread-eagled, firmly tied—struggle was useless.

Manion came over and put his ugly fat face down close to her and whispered, "You, Sandra, are so beautiful. Even in those awful khaki combat clothes I could tell your beauty. If it were not sacrilege, I would have this honor, but alas you are the Goddess,

160

and must be mated with the Renquist."

He stood up, and in a strong voice said, "You, Sandra, goddess-consort of the Renquist, must now be strapped — with the sacred whip."

"No, wait — why?"

"Do you not know why? A cloud of forgetfulness must have passed over you on the surface, oh Goddess. You must be strapped, and severely. The chances of bearing a male child will be increased by the pain — that is why. It is the way . . ."

A gong was sounded by Manion.

Thus was the Amazon-like Freefighter prepared for what was to come. Her winsome body firmly secured, exposed to whatever whim the priest and his cohorts had in mind.

"Let the ceremony of the Blessed Honeymoon night begin," the high priest intoned. "Cut her clothing from her."

*"No."*

The two handmaidens took small knives and quickly snipped off the flimsy bra and bikini bottom from the struggling bound redhead.

Thus stripped of the last shred of protection, Rona's upthrust backside, spread wide by her ankle bindings, revealed the deep crease between her firm tan thighs. Every detail of her female anatomy was exposed in the most lascivious way. Many a male would have yielded to the temptation of plunging his manhood between her startlingly full and jutting posterior globes. But the high priest and the soldier-monks — aside from their viewing it as sacrilege to take from Renquist what was his — were likewise sexually incapable. Only the ritual concerned them. All

161

the nuptial rules must be observed; their God, Renquist, must have his honeymoon privilege. Through the sacrament of the insertion of the snake-rod.

"Let it commence," Manion solemnly intoned. "Now, before the sacred impregnation, the chastisement must be rendered."

She shouted, "You can't do this."

Manion went to a dark recess of the room and returned holding a long slender whip, the kind formerly used to hasten reluctant carriage horses. He tested the long cord in the air. It snapped viciously in the darkness near her body.

"Oh no, please, don't."

The second blow was for her. Heeding not her entreaties, Manion moved into action. The long birch rod swished viciously down across Rona's pinioned posterior. She let out a cry as the sudden blow stung across her bottom, sideways.

"Stop. No. Oh God, it *hurts*," Rona shouted. Before she could say another thing, the leather cord swished down again, and then a third time. She screamed out as much in anger and frustration as in pain, and she frantically wiggled her backside in a vain attempt to avoid the blows.

A dozen telling strokes placed expertly from her lower back to the tensed thighs followed, and then Manion started the whip blows back up towards her back once more. Rona cursed and strained at her bindings, twisting in a frenzy every time a blow was launched, but to no avail. Why were they doing this to her? Why? She screamed as loud as she could, which was plenty loud, every time a telling blow of the rod was delivered. Maybe somebody would hear, maybe Rockson was looking for her. He would, he would come—somebody *had to come*.

Manion paused to inspect his handiwork. And was pleased. Sandra's tightly stretched nether-globes were crisscrossed with red weal marks. Hardly an inch of her firm flesh had escaped the horizontal scourges he'd delivered.

Now it was time to change position and deliver the vertical blows. The job would not be over, and the Goddess not properly prepared for her sacred trust, until there was a red crosshatch pattern on her lovely posterior.

The blows began anew, this time up and down. They fell so many times in the next few minutes that Rona thought she was going to be beaten to death.

On the hundreth blow, a dizzy, half-conscious Rona heard Manion say, "The scourging is over." Manion turned to the statue and bowed. "Oh, Renquist, your bride is properly chastised. As it was written, pain and the anger aroused in a chastised bride will increase the chance that a male child will be born of this sacred union. So be it. Now let the insemination proceed."

Rona twisted her head, shook the blurriness from her eyes. What were they doing over there? They were chanting and moving about the statue of the snake. Oh God, they don't mean to—

"Praise be to Renquist," the acolytes, the handmaidens, and the soldiers shouted. The two maroon-robed acolytes went forward from the group of chanters, over to the ice-covered votary that was the carved cobra snake. They took up flickering torches and played the flames under the snake statue's head

163

to gradually melt the ice seal around the long, slender cylindrical object that was hidden in the snake's stone mouth. Slowly, once the long cylinder was freed of its ice, the torches were played along its bottom, until the frost was burned away. The sixteen-inch-long green glass tube was a straight glass snake, a sealed catheter with a milky fluid in its narrow interior.

"The honeymoon vessel has been prepared," Manion intoned, ringing the gong again. "Let the insemination of the honeymoon begin."

*Insemination?* "No," Rona gasped, twisting her tear-stained yet defiant countenance around to see the green glass vial as it was passed to Manion's meaty hands.

*No.*

Rockson had heard the frantic screams for several minutes, and had run at all the speed he could muster, setting himself far ahead of his companions. Rona was being tortured—somewhere in this maze of tunnels. He went up two dead ends, and then retracing his steps, tried a third tunnel. And found the snake temple. He blasted the door open with a burst of fire—explosive 9mm bullets from his Liberator auto-fire rifle tearing the huge brass doors off their hinges.

Rockson burst into the Temple of the Snake, and immediately took in the situation.

The priests. Rona—bound and naked, the long green-glass cylinder poised between her spread legs. The awful streaks of red across her backside.

He leveled his weapon on the man with the vial, the one closest to Rona.

164

"Drop whatever the hell you're holding, mister, or die."

McCaughlin and Chen flew into the doorway behind him, to back up his words. The soldier-monks around the temple who had started to lift their weapons were cut down by a sweep of hot lead from three Liberator rifles; their bodies jerked back and slammed against the altar of their false god, spurting hot streams of blood.

The blue-robed man at Rona's side dropped the glass vial and it shattered at his feet.

Detroit came in next, shotpistol up. Ready. Danik, panting from the run, came in behind him. It was a tense moment. They were in time to hear Rockson yell, "Away from her, priest."

Manion made to reach the trank-stick on his belt — and never made it. Rockson fired on full automatic. The priest's head, severed by a sweep of hot lead, spun across the darkness. The body that had belonged to Manion's head sank to the floor like a sack of potatoes, the neck-opening pumping out a fountain of blood.

Through the cordite smoke of the weapons, the Doomsday Warrior stepped over to his beloved. Rockson approached the beaten nude figure stretched out on the mound with trepidation. Was she alive? Yes. But her eyes were bleary.

"Rona, are you—"

"Untie me, Rock," she groaned in a soft voice.

Rockson used his balisong knife to cut the bindings off. He threw his coat over her, she zipped it up. It was large and went down halfway to her knees. It would do. Detroit was stripping the headless corpse of its shoes—they were about right for Rona's feet. Rockson slipped them on her and lifted her to him and hugged her, "Rona, are you—"

"I'm basically all right, though I don't want to spend any time sitting real soon."

She had spunk. That was for sure.

"Can you walk?"

"Walk? Hell, I can run. Let's get out of here."

There wasn't much left of the enemy down the long ice corridor, Rona quickly saw that. Slumped bodies were everywhere. The Freefighters had gotten only so far in their Cultist disguises, and had finished off a good number of their enemy on the way to rescue Rona.

Rockson had grabbed one of the surviving soldier-monks from the temple and was pushing him along the corridor, a gun in his back. "You find us the passageway to Eden—the old construction tunnel—or else."

"The construction tunnel? Why, that was blown up, sealed off last week. There is no way to Eden anymore."

Rockson spun the cowed man around on his heels, and cocked the shotpistol and placed its cold barrel against the captive's forehead. "Then, you find us another passageway to Eden."

# Chapter 18

The captive, the pupils of his colorless eyes pinned in fright, stuttered out, "There—there is a passage—to the Caverns of H-Hell. They say th-that those caverns come out in—in Eden. But—"

Rockson said, "You take us to this passage—*now.*"

The captive complied, leading them down a series of corridors, then down some steps with an inch of dust on them. "God, Rock," said Detroit, "no one must have been down here for a long, long time."

"That's because," Danik gasped, keeping up the pace down the curving wide stairs with great effort,"—because the Caverns of Hell have legends of horror."

They reached the bottom of the stairs; their flashlights played along a wide crack in a stone wall. There was darkness beyond, and a cool wind coming from the hole. "This is it," said the captive. Now let me go—you said . . ."

Rockson let go of the man's arm. "Get the hell out of here, jerk, and don't tell anyone—"

"I won't," the man yelled, taking off back up the

stairs two steps at a time.

"Now, what's the story on these caverns, Danik?"

"In Eden we know them as the place of horrors. A natural series of caves with strange voices in them — and death. The man that led us here was correct, though. They do come out in Eden. Through a fissure. It isn't sealed because a fresh wind comes from it. The whole ecosystem of Eden would overload if they closed the fissure. The Caverns of Hell — sometimes called the air caves — were briefly explored by early Edenites. Most never returned. The few that did told of horror beyond the imagination."

"What sorts of horrors? You mentioned voices — could just be echoes, coming back long after someone spoke. What else?"

"I read that there were animals — of some sort — they had big teeth. Adults in Eden never read of such oddities, it was just nursery-school stuff. I don't really know."

"Maybe," ventured McCaughlin, "they just made up the tales. The leaders of Eden weren't too keen about having people go out of the city. Could be all hogwash."

"Hogwash or not," Rockson said, "I hear some thundering feet up the stairwell. I think the reinforcements are coming. Shall we make the plunge?"

Rockson was sure the Death City folks wouldn't follow. He was right. They were unmolested in their quick march through the cavern. Danik told him that if they just kept going south, they would descend steeply, and then go up after seven miles and come

168

out at Eden. A piece of cake. Of course he was going by dim recollections of a map he'd seen in a book in Eden — when he was a child. They found direction with one of Schecter's pocket compasses; unaffected by local sources of magnetism, the nifty little luminous dial-thing unerringly pointed magnetic north.

When they had gotten about a quarter mile into their remarkable passage, there was a tremendous rumble, and rocks and soot sifted down from the trembling mountain above them.

"Quick, against the wall of stalagmites over there," Rock ordered.

Because they obeyed their leader, they avoided anything more than a few shoulder scrapes from falling chunks of rock. The rumble died down. Then its echo also. All was silent.

"What was that?" Rona asked.

"There's your answer," Rockson declared, pointing back toward where they had come from. There was smoke and dust exuding from the crevice they had entered the cavern from.

"The entranceway to Death City has been blown up," Detroit surmised grimly.

"There's no turning back now," McCaughlin stated flatly. "It's forward or die."

They proceeded on their way, on a sloping but secure floor of limestone. It was a beautiful underground vista opening before them, a limestone cavern, with stalagmites of every shape and color — they were amazed at the beauty of the delicate formations when they shone their lights on the dim shapes.

All seemed well, and then the pleasantly cool temperature rose. It became quite warm. "Some sort of hot lava bed perhaps, ahead." said Scheransky, an expert on such matters.

"I sure hope this is the right cavern," Rona said.

No one commented on that hope. It had to be the right cavern. Or they were dead.

The air became fetid with sulfurous fumes, but was still breathable. They unclicked their flashlights as the light of a bubbling magma stream off to their left illuminated the way for another half mile. Then the air and temperature returned to normal. "Good thing that stream of hot lava wasn't in our way," Detroit said. "I'm not much for fire walking."

Now instead of heat, it was cold—bitter cold. And the pebble-littered path among the rock formations descended steeply. It was cautious going, each Freefighter helping the next twist and turn down the escarpment. Worse, here and there were human bones—skulls with huge dead eyesockets, fragments of clothing of the twentieth-century variety.

"No one has to be told to keep alert, do they?"

At Rockson's suggestion, they went single file. "I sure wish we had some rope—I don't like groping in the—" Rock stopped in his tracks. The lightbeam from his flashlight had reached some object ahead. A big hump of rock. It stood out on the flatness that lay, thankfully, just ahead. Their steep, dangerous descent was over.

They came down one by one to the flatness. Then onward they marched, braving whatever would come before them. After all, it was incredible that they had gotten as far as they had—perhaps Rockson's mutant luck would take them all the way to Eden after all, and thence to a safe return to Colorado.

Rona had swallowed some of the pain pills and antibiotics from Chen's belt-pouch supply of medicinals. She was keeping up, despite her injuries.

"That landmark, guys, let's head for it." Rock said, referring to the hump of rock about a hundred yards ahead. "We'll climb atop it and take a look around, combining all our lights."

The walk to the rock hummock took no time at all. They found it to be about a hundred feet high. Steep, but walkable. When they reached its rounded summit, their combined lights could find the cavern ceiling above, about another hundred feet up. It was studded with long color-radiant crystal stalactites. Rockson took another look at his special compass. "We're still on track. Must have come a third of the way, and there hasn't been any monsters," he reassured.

"Still, it's a big cave, and we have a way to go," Detroit said.

Rockson had the party play their lights over the inky distance. Finally he saw something other than a smooth floor. Something white — another long hill of some sort. "Might as well head that way," Rock said, "it's almost due south. It looks like it's man-made."

Again into the lower darkness they plunged. They came to the white object. It wasn't a hill, it was a handmade wall of immense stones. Atop the ten-foot wall, which went on into the darkness in both directions, completely cutting off their trek, there were writings. And a cryptic set of drawings. The words were in Spanish.

Detroit played the torch up to the dusty script. "Yes, it's Spanish. I'll translate. It says, 'Beyond here dwell the ones whose mere whispered words destroy the mind. Better to kill yourself now than to proceed through these halls and have your mind tortured.' It's signed 'Father Serra.' "

"I'm for turning back," Danik said, with a distinct tremble in his voice. "And go where?" Scheransky retorted.

"What the hell does that warning mean?" McCaughlin asked.

"I'm not sure," said Rock, "but the inscription is really old and the dust on the floor has no footprints in it. This way has not been entered for decades, maybe even for centuries. Perhaps it was written by some early explorer who somehow got into these deep caverns. There might have been some exits to the surface long ago. But the wall was built by many hands. And machinery. Whatever is on the other side, well, it might be dead by now. In any case we're climbing over."

"Hold on, guys," Detroit said. He had wandered down the wall a bit. "There's more wording here—something abut—" he rubbed the stones with his hands, "something about 'the Whisperers use the power of your own mind against you . . . what is a nightmare becomes real. Guard well your mind but no matter how you resist, the madness comes . . .' That's all I can make out. And by the way there's another skeleton down here—he has a chisel in his hand. I'd say this fellow made the inscription."

"Doesn't anyone want to go back?" pleaded Danik. His plea was ignored.

"All of us should remember our meditative training," Chen admonished. "There is the power of the

172

*chi*, the inner force within, to protect us. Let us be brave and confident."

"Chen is right, we will proceed," Rockson said, starting to drive the mini mountain-climbing pitons he'd brought along in his beltpack into the wall with his baton handle. When he had climbed halfway up, he had Detroit pass the reluctant Class Act up and put her atop the wall. Detroit climbed up and stood on the two-foot-wide top with the dog, scanning the darkness with the electron binoculars, his rifle ready to protect them all. Rockson climbed down the other side, putting more of the pitons in the wall to accomplish that. The other Freefighters were over in a minute, using the strong metal mini-spikes as hand- and footholds. Detroit handed the heavy wolf-dog down, and then climbed down himself.

Class Act ran forward in the darkness, sniffing and growling softly.

The Freefighters moved off behind the canine mutant, guns ready. All except for Archer, who had his crossbow out and the biggest steel arrow notched.

"Wait," the frightened Edenite implored, "I'm coming."

Smokestone muttered, "I sense something. The dog is right to growl. There is a presence . . ."

The party had no choice but to move on, though with heightened trepidation. They passed bizarre stalactites, twisted funnels tapering to a sharp point fifty or sixty feet above them, a veritable sea of giant pinpoints. The air was freezing now, the ground beneath them slippery with frost. And there was a new element — sounds.

"Is anybody breathing funny?" Detroit was the first

173

to ask. They all said they were breathing the same as always.

"Perhaps," suggested Chen, "it is merely an echo from the stalagmites."

"No, I definitely hear some funny breathing," Detroit insisted, stopping again after another hundred paces. "And I hear — voices — over there." He shot his beam to the left, and their beams followed. Nothing. Just oddly shaped gray-blue rocks.

A case of nerves?

They moved onward. They left the flat plain; the way was now inclined upward. "We're halfway," Rock muttered.

Detroit Green, a man of easy mind, relaxed and always optimistic, was surprisingly the first to fall under the spell of the deadly illusions created by "the Whisperers." He fell into the dream easily. First there was just a dull hum, an electricity in the dark cold air of the underground passage. It was just the whisper of a gentle soft voice, a breeze, the hint of fingers tracing over the forehead. And with that slight mental breeze, cold soft fingers reached into his mind. Not with horror. Not at first. Just gentle pleasant memories.

Thus the unseen beings, the Whisperers, that created the illusions were able to painlessly enter Detroit's mind undetected, unopposed. He had steeled himself for horror. And there wasn't any.

He was suddenly basking in the warm sunlight of a gentle spring day near Century City. Detroit Green saw not the darkness of the cavern, felt not its icy wind. Instead he was in the verdant forest of poplars and cottonwoods. The leaves on the trees overhead made the sunlight flicker in his eyes as he walked unafraid and happy toward his loved ones. He had a nice musk deer he had killed draped over his shoulder — he was happy.

And now that the Whisperers had entered his mind by this devious trick, the images changed. The deer became a desiccated rotted corpse, foul and crawling with worms. He shouted and dropped it. He saw the trees around him wither, and the leaves rot off and fall in a cascade of dank death. The sky opened up with blacks snow swirling down, burning his skin . . .

The Whisperers were picking up his most fearful thoughts — like black acid snow — and projecting them back on him.

Detroit tried to throw it off, started chanting his words of protection, as Chen had taught. He caught a glimpse for an instant of his real surroundings. Detroit stood still. He tried to gain control. He stated, "No — no, I am here, I am in the cavern — " But the brave Freefighter, despite his best effort, couldn't hold the thought, and reality slipped away again.

He was suddenly in boot camp, a raw recruit to the Freefighter cause. A bull-necked DI jabbed him in the belly with a finger and said, "All right, Green, you have to prove yourself. Jump down this little hole. It's not deep. You can do it. The others did. They'll laugh at you if — "

"I can do it, I can . . ." Detroit prepared to jump. It wasn't deep — just six or seven feet. It was easy.

175

"Hey, what is Detroit up to? What's he doing over there by that crevice?" Rock said, shining the light over to the man.

"The illusions have him," Chen shouted. "Quickly, let's get him."

Detroit was poised on the edge of the cliff. The two Freefighters ran to him, and Rockson tackled him and rolled his friend from the abyss. Detroit struggled with the Doomsday Warrior, screaming and tearing at the man as if he were an enemy. He saw not his compatriot trying to save him, but rather the snaking tendrils of a bloodfruit plant. In the illusion projected by the Whisperers, the tendrils had locked around his legs and wouldn't let go. He searched for his knife, but Chen seized it away from him.

Rockson got Detroit in a hammerlock, and as Rona slapped his face repeatedly, the illusion-mad Freefighter gradually ceased his struggle and came around.

He sat there exhausted, his chest heaving. "Rock — if you could see what I saw, you'd understand. Sorry, I —"

Rockson slapped him on the back. "Forget it. But tell us how it got you — weren't you guarding?"

Detroit told Rock and the other how it had used a gentle, pleasant memory to get into his mind.

"So that's what happened. Everyone — keep counting or saying a mantra as you walk, don't reminisce about anything, don't let your minds wander. *Now let's get out of here.*"

They went on. Rockson felt the subtlest of mental attack. It was a pleasant thought about sitting in the restaurant at Century City and ordering a drink of —

*no*. He fended it off, shutting his mind like a steel spring on it—it passed.

Rona broke stride momentarily, then she too threw it off. One by one they were tested and found not wanting. Thanks to Detroit's warning.

But with Scheransky it was a different story. Scheransky had trouble remembering his mantra, so he counted. One—two—three. It worked well for a time, his mind didn't wander, he was keeping up with the others. Perhaps his lack of deep meditative training, he had trouble with such things—didn't matter. He would be all right. But that wasn't the case.

They had gone perhaps another three hundred yards in the darkness, when Scheransky suddenly heard his voice, his counting of numbers in Russian, suddenly change to the voice of another man. It was the voice of a guard, a KGB guard. He was a child standing in the snow of the Gulag Reception Station. He was next to his father, a proud prison official. And the counting was not of footsteps in the dark cavern, but the counting of half-naked prisoners walking by him.

Each time a prisoner walked by, his father made a mark in a little notebook. It was so long ago. It was the day that Scheransky most wanted to forget. The day that haunted him.

The Russian's most dreaded memory was buried deep in his unconscious childhood memories. But the deeper the fear, the more hidden it was, the easier it was for the Whisperers to use it . . . and the more horrible and real it seemed when it came to mind.

There he was in the cold winter darkness of the gulag. And there was a purge going on, the sixth in a year. In the Kremlin, the Malenkov forces were out, and the Dzernoviks' faction was in, meaning new prisoners were arriving by the trainload—prisoners who had endured month after month of torture already at the hands of the KGB.

And as the faceless political prisoners walked by, one was not anonymous. One, just one, was not a thing to be reviled.

"*Momma.*" Scheransky gasped. "What are you—"

The woman, number 412, wore a torn and ragged filthy striped robe. She had bare feet, blood in the cracks of her frozen toes, staining the snow beneath her. She stopped, looked glazed at him, looking as if he were a rock or building.

"Momma, it's me." He turned to his father, pulled on his arm, "Poppa, it's Momma, it's her—why is she here with the guilty? Why is she dressed like this, why is she with the prisoners?"

His father's face was ashen, his swollen chest suddenly deflated. His black beady eyes grew wide with horror. It was her. "I cannot do anything," he whispered close to the boy's ear, and he dragged little Totu Scheransky away. The boy Scheransky was screaming, "Momma, Momma."

"Shut up, stupid," his father insisted, "she is not your mother—not anymore. She is a traitor, I don't know what she did, but she did it. And we don't know her . . ."

"But Momma—"

His father slapped him. He fell face first in the snow and he heard the *crunch crunch crunch* of the naked feet of the prisoners walking listlessly across the snow toward the unheated confinement building.

Scheransky, though lost in the illusion, continued walking with his compatriots in the cavern. He was saying, "No, Poppa, no, it *is* Momma . . . it is . . . it is . . ." In his ears rang the whistle of the death train as it slowly pulled out. The *crunch crunch* of the Freefighters' boots was, in his mind, the *crunch crunch* of the political prisoners' bare feet toward the death house.

But that was not the worst—that was a past reality. A long-ago memory unearthed by the powers of the unseen enemy in the cavern. Now came the dreaded fantasy:

Suddenly Scheransky was stopped dead in his tracks. And dimly in the cavern's deep recesses he heard his mother's voice, all cracked and trembling horribly. "Son, son," she pleaded. "My little Totu, why did you let them take me away? Why did you deny me, your mother?"

"I didn't—Mother, I—I—I'm sorry," Scheransky stuttered out. "I—"

Then the words choked off in his throat, for out of the darkness stepped the decayed, twisted dry corpse of his mother, still wearing the tattered moldy robe with the black stripes of a prisoner on it. She lifted her dried fungus-covered hand in the half-light and shook her finger at him. "Bad boy, you're a very bad boy."

"No," he aspirated, his breath frozen, his chest hard and tight. "I—"

"You let them kill me. You did. You denied me—and now—" the fungus-caked dissolving corpse's dry mouth cracked a toothy smile—"now, Son, *I've come to get you* . . .

"Join . . . me . . . in . . . cemetery. Here, come . . . kiss your mother . . ." The corpse lurched forward, smacking its dead brown lips over teeth that fell out as she moved.

"No . . . please . . . don't come any closer." Scheransky screamed, but he was unable to back off. The corpse kept coming closer. "Oh God Jesus," Scheransky cried, "Keep her away — keep it away from me."

Scheransky brought his hands up to his face but not in time. For the staggering mother-corpse leapt at him and held him in a bony-hard death grip. She started biting his face with her decayed teeth, which shattered and broke into sharp fragments as they stuck into his skin. "No —" he screamed, "*noooooooooooo.*"


"What's the matter with Scheransky?" Rock yelled as he ran back to the Russian. Scheransky was screaming and tearing at the air as if he was being attacked. Rock and Detroit, who reached their companion at the same time, grabbed his arms. Rockson shouted, shook the Russian defector. "Scheransky, it's not real, not real. Whatever is happening is an *illusion.*"

Slowly the screams died down, the flailing and crying died down. Finally Scheransky just sat there on the cold cavern floor, on his haunches, sobbing softly, "Mother . . . Mother, God, I —"

Rockson gently lifted his friend to his feet. "It's all over now . . . The nightmare is over. We have to go, come on, come on . . . left . . . right . . . left . . . That's it."

There was no more mental attack. And there came a different voice, a voice so soft you could sense it rather than hear it. "We are sorry," said the whisper, "we thought you were more . . . of the bad ones. The ones we kill. But your hearts are good. We are sorry . . . sorry . . . sorry . . ."

And there was silence. They were left — except for one more sentence from the darkness that warned: "Beware of the sky . . . sky . . . sky . . ."

After assessing the damage — no one was seriously hurt, either mentally or physically, though they were still reeling from what had happened, Rockson urged them onward.

# Chapter 19

At last they entered a snaking, twisting portion of the cavern with beautiful crystalline stalactites dangling down at them, and the hum in the air, that hum that was the power of the whisperers, ceased. And no one felt those icy fingers reaching into their minds anymore—they had made it.

They spent a dreary hour shivering and walking in what they hoped was the right direction, toward a spiral-shaped immense stalactite hanging from the murky darkness above. The compass said it was dead south. Rock hoped it was right. They had come two thirds of the way now.

There was the faintest squeak of leather wings against cold air. And suddenly there was not illusion—but swift real death. The Grim Reaper—in the form of a giant swooping bat—came at them screeching, and its clawed feet squeezed about Smokestone before anyone reacted. He was lifted into the darkness. "Shoot, shoot," he yelled. "Never mind if you hit me."

Rockson understood. The man was in pain, in the grip of a prehistoric creature of darkness. And he reacted. Rock sprayed the air with explosive bullets in the direction of the voice. There was a shriek, a nonhuman shriek. He stopped firing. And waited. There was a tremendous thud a moment later, about a hundred yards to their east.

No one had to tell the rest to follow Rockson through the Stygian darkness, playing their bright flashbeams about to find their lost Indian companion.

They found Smokestone lying crumpled on the hard rocks. He had blood seeping out of two huge wounds, one on either side of his ribcage. Chen immediately went down on his knees and pulled back the torn material of the chief's garments. He turned his face up to Rockson and slowly shook his head. No. He was not going to make it.

There were no bullet holes on the chief; Rock was thankful for that. The major damage was from the creature itself, though it was obvious that Smokestone's leg bones were broken too.

The Indian chief was beckoning with his one good hand for Rock to come closer; his lips moved.

Rock put his ear right next to the bleeding lips of his companion and listened. The chief whispered, "Please . . . cut out my eyes, after—after I die . . . bury them on the surface in the light . . . of the sun . . ."

The chief looked pleadingly into Rock's eyes. Asking for understanding. Rockson understood. It was the Indian way. To have your eyes buried in the darkness of night would condemn your soul to wander in the afterlife, homeless and tortured. Rockson said, "I will do it." The Chief half-smiled, then exhaled but did not inhale again.

Rockson told the others to move back, and then he did the work with the knife, putting Smokestone's eyes in his belt-pouch for transport, eventually, to the surface.

Chen had his explosive star-dart out and was poised with it. Detroit scanned the darkness above with the electron night-binoculars. This was done while the Freefighters and Danik rolled some rocks atop the body. Then Rockson recited a brief Indian prayer:

"Great Spirit, you are everything, the first and the always. Through you your children have strong hearts and they walk in the straight path in a sacred manner.

"This fallen chief has walked the sacred path of beauty. His heart was continually yours. Take him to your sky dwelling, for there this beautiful man belongs. I will do my part to let his eyes see your light."

# Chapter 20

Rockson ordered that only one flashlight be aimed forward; the rest were swept above them, to at least give some warning should another of the bats come to snatch another of their company away. None came. Class Act was hunkered down on her haunches, as if ashamed that she hadn't caught the scent of the thing that swooped to kill. Rock said, "It's okay, dog. We didn't notice either. If anything," he said, stopping to pet the dog, "it was my fault. I didn't heed the warning of the Whisperers. Whoever they are, they tried to warn us about the bat."

Chen overheard, and said, "Rock, you saved Smokestone from the jaws of that thing—and yet you blame yourself for his death. Don't do that. It happens. Evidently the Whisperers aren't our enemy. They thought we were someone else. We all heard their warnings, and yet we didn't do anything. Blame all of us."

Rock stood up and continued walking. "I'm in charge. It was my responsibility he died."

The gloomy self-reproach was broken by events. They came to a second artificial wall of stone, this one of gray granite, and cruder than the first. It ran for about ten meters, and was so low you could step over it. Why was this one built? What could be held back by such a wall?

Perhaps it was built only to draw attention to the message it held, Rockson concluded. This wall had an inscription also. This time it was in English. Rock did the honors:

"It says, '*Ahead are the Eight Legs of Death.*' That's all it says."

No one hazarded a guess as to what that meant.

The cavern ceiling became lower as they proceeded. They were all glad of that and of the long sharp stalactites that hung down, practically joining their like formations that jutted from the floor of the lower cavern.

"The bat can't fly in here," Rock said happily. "We've entered a smaller cavern."

And more surprising, they soon entered a wide ten-foot-high corridor hewn out of the rock of the mountain, leaving the cavern and heading upward at a steep angle. "The path to Eden, finally," the much-shook-up Danik said.

"I think," observed Rockson, sweeping his beam about, "that this area has been fortified, perhaps to be earthquake proof. There's very little fallen debris on the floor. Someone wanted this area to be safe— perhaps there was something here they wanted to protect."

They headed onward, feeling somehow more secure to have entered an man-made area. Surely Eden couldn't be far away now.

Chen put down his explosive shuriken and Rona lowered her Liberator rifle. The giant bat was behind them.

"Sure a relief," Rock said, lowering his shotpistol. "I was sure we would be attacked again by the bat if we stayed in the cavern."

The minute he said that, however, Rockson's mutant sense of danger sent a shot of adrenaline through his body.

On a hunch, he played his flashbeam to the right. There was something square standing in the darkness. Several crates. Each about five feet wide.

Detroit had caught them in his light too. He cautiously walked over to one, shotpistol at the ready. He announced that the crates were broken open, and that there were scrape marks on the ground around them, as if something had been dragged off.

Rockson came over and stood by Detroit. He examined the ordinary-looking wooden crates. They were made of brittle boards. Cheap wood, and easy to break. But they were covered with fine dust. Perhaps they were a hundred or so years old. Some abandoned supplies from Eden, he ventured.

Rock noticed that most of the crates were overturned, and further inspection proved all were empty, their plastic-bubble-foam insulation scattered about like they had been unpacked with a frenzy.

"Hey, Rock," said McCaughlin. "What's Scabies?"

"Scabies? They're little mites—microscopic actually. A parasite like fleas or lice. Sometimes they get into your skin if you don't bathe—cause a whole lot of itching. Only way to kill them is with a special

189

soap. Lots of the underclass in the Soviet fortress-cities are crawling with the nasty little buggers. Why?"

"These packing crates are marked S.C.A.-B.I.E.S.—must be some acronym."

Rockson played his light up and down the crates. "In the twentieth century the military was crazy about acronyms. They called Browning Automatic Rifles B.A.R.S., they called the Strategic Air Command S.A.C., and so on."

"Yeah," said Detroit, "but what's S.C.A.-B.I.E.S.?"

"Here it is," said Rona. "One of the packages has a lot of small stencil writing on it—and the answer: Special Computerized Ambulatory Bombs Intended for Enemy Systems. So that's what were in here—some sort of war supplies."

"Probably left here by some of the founders of Eden—hmm . . ." Rockson said, lost in thought. "Something about scabies . . .

"Of course," Rockson yelled. "Scabies are tiny spiders. 'Beware of the eight-legged ones.' That means beware of the spiders—or scabies. They have eight legs, too."

Detroit took out his shotpistol and looked around, expecting something. He didn't know what to expect, but something was going to happen.

"Hey, Rock," Rona said, from further up the corridor. "Come look at this."

She had called them over to see the deep gouges in the floor of the corridor.

"Craters, each a foot wide, and as deep. Old also."

"What made them? There's a half-dozen."

190

"The result of some sort of artillery shell explosions, I guess." Detroit said.

The black Freefighter, an expert at such things as determining the power of an explosive by its blast effect, examined the craters more carefully. There were pieces of shrapnel and bits of bones in them — bones long calcified by the damp dankness of the cavern.

"Whatever blew up here was aimed at some human beings. I'd say these explosions happened a long time ago, though," Detroit said.

They had proceeded less than five minutes more and were still in the wide low-ceilinged corridor when there was a whirring sound and the distinct *plip-plop* of a hundred tiny metal feet.

And indeed they were hearing correctly. Caught in a half-dozen flashbeams, the slowly advancing horde of three-foot-high eight-legged walking bombs from the twentieth century approached, their white sensor antennae extended above their round headless bodies, tracking their prey. They were beeping happily, their atomic-cell batteries feeding them the power to move their sharp clawlike legs. They had found victims at last.

"Prepare to fire, Freefighters. The SCABIES are coming." Rock said, crouching with his Liberator forward.

"No. Don't shoot," implored Detroit in a hoarse whisper. "I've studied twentieth-century weapons — these things have hearing sensors — they are intended, I think, for enemy tanks. They crawl onto them and blow up. They probably crawl up on anything that makes noises. Like those people that they made into bone fragments back there. In the craters. See how they're just moving around at random? The clunk of our boots is what attracted them to us. If we just don't make any mechanical noises — or fire our weapons — they might stop."

"Let's follow Detroit's advice, gang," Rock said. "I have the feeling they're pretty well armored anyway. Bullets probably wouldn't do much good. Let's move on quietly, and see what happens."

Indeed the metal creature-bombs paused in their tracks once the Freefighters were silent. Their little antennae spun this way and that, searching for a noise.

"Who activated them?" Rona whispered.

"Maybe no one. My guess is an earthquake toppled the crates," said Rock, "and when the crates fell, some must have rolled out and hit their power-on switches on something. Let's slowly move out, keeping our weapons trained on them — you first, Rona."

But the instant she moved, so did the leader among the metal death machines. Rona froze in her tracks. "What now?" she asked. "They seem to follow movement too."

"No, the echo in the corridor is amplifying our footfalls," Detroit said. "They will follow us, try to catch us — but see how slow they move? Like crabs more than ants. Their batteries must be run-down. After a century, why wouldn't they be?"

"Yeah, maybe we can outrun them, or maybe we should just shoot 'em to pieces," McCaughlin snarled out.

"We'll try to run up the corridor. They might not have the energy to follow . . . Quickly, along the left

192

wall, out of their way. Everyone—let's *go*."

But such an easy escape was not to be. The minute they took off, running as fast as they could, the insidious metal things took after them, bleeping and grinding on ancient gears but still moving rapidly. They came after the humans like voracious insects that had spotted fresh meat. Whatever powered the little metal hell-things still propelled them faster than a man—or woman—could run.

Chen, who was in the rear, tossed several exploding shurikens accurately over his shoulder as he took flight, and they made their targets. But the metal things absorbed the explosive force of the deadly star-knives, and once they righted themselves from their fallen-over positions, they kept coming.

The most the martial-arts master's weapons did was knock several on their bellies momentarily.

"Spread out so you don't hit each other, and fire back whenever you see one getting close to you," Rockson ordered. He crouched and, turning, himself blasted back accurately with a withering barrage of 9mm death. Then he fired six explosive shells from his shotpistol.

The shiny metal things were blasted off their feet, but the bullets zinged off their extra-hard shells into the darkness. And again they righted themselves and kept coming. A quick play of the light behind showed hundreds, maybe thousands, of the tough little monsters.

"We'll have to think of something else to stop them," Rock yelled over the barrage of fire pouring out of the Freefighters' weapons.

"I've got an idea," Scheransky said. "We throw

193

some of our stuff — clothes, anything, behind us. They grab it and blow themselves up. Let them destroy themselves if we can't do it."

"I'll never say anything against borscht again," Rock said. "A brilliant idea. Everyone — take off up the corridor. But discard some items of clothing — anything."

Chen threw down his souvenir of the battles in Death City — the odd helmet he'd snatched from the Snake Temple soldier. It rolled toward the little beeping followers.

A flashbeam — Detroit's — shot back to reveal two of the little nasties pouncing upon it and wrapping their little steel legs about the helmet's circumference. Then they blew up. Pieces of metal flew everywhere, one catching Chen in the shoulder.

Rockson encouraged the runners to continue the discarding of materials. There had to be some limit to the numbers of the metal scabies, he figured.

Within minutes the near-exhausted sprinters had nothing save their clothing and weapons to discard behind them. And Rockson knew they couldn't keep up the pace much longer. Danik was near his limit for sure.

Rockson, concerned for the others, should have paid more attention to his own bootheels. A particularly well functioning scabie-bomb was suddenly upon him. It scurried up to hold fast to his left boot, almost tripping him. It was beeping faster and faster. It was going to explode.

# Chapter 21

He winced in pain as the sharp crablike legs of the ambulatory bomb seized his foot in their crushing grip. He tore at his bootlaces and pulled out of the boot, thus leaving the death-maker behind. He ran onward, sharp rocks on the floor of the corridor ripping at his bare foot; still he was catching up to the Freefighters, who were cheering him on, urging him to get away from the thing before—

*Boom.* The thing that had grabbed his boot exploded. And more of the beastly bugs came pouring through its smoke.

The Freefighters poured their combined fire on the little menaces that were closest to catching up to Rockson, but one of the steel-legged hell-things put on a burst of battery-driven speed and climbed onto his calf and sunk its steel-tipped legs into his flesh. He fell, and tore at it; he could hear the soft ticking grow louder, the beeping grow more intense as he pried at the many legs of steel.

The Freefighters were hanging back, desperate to help. "Go on, don't wait for me." It was a direct order and obeyed by all—except for Class Act. Class Act, snarling and with its triple row of steely teeth exposed

195

to the full, leapt out of the nearby darkness and plunged against the tenacious machine-creature. The loyal wolf-dog furiously tore at the lethal walking bomb, succeeding in tearing it from Rockson's leg. Then the dog itself became the target of the relentless steel claws. The metal mandibles locked around the belly of the beast. Class Act, howling like a hound of hell itself, ran off into the Stygian blackness.

There was a blast. Bits of raw, red dog flesh and fur pelt were thrown at Rockson as he painfully rose to his feet.

Rockson painfully limped along after his companions. The loyal sled dog had given him his life back.

Detroit was lobbing grenade after grenade behind Rock, having set the pineapples on slow fuse. Some were grabbed and held by the bombs, other blew up by themselves.

Archer came up to Rockson and lifted the injured man and threw him over his shoulder. They took off again up the corridor.

When the hell, thought Rockson through a veil of pain, would they reach Eden? Would the damned killer claws follow them into it even if they did reach their goal?

Danik, his legs or breath having given out, fell. McCaughlin swept him up and carried him easily.

Rock's leg was torn in two places; a sharp pain jolted him at every step of the giant man holding him.

It was not just his own problem—or Danik's. It was obvious—they could no longer outrun the ambulatory arsenal. They would have to make a stand.

Rockson, from his awkward position, was able to see ahead. He saw a place to make a stand.

"Quick, behind those barrels ahead."

The Freefighters, exhausted and about to give out, dove behind the barrels and took up positions, crouching or full out flat in the spaces between the round black containers. Their weapons, already half out of ammo, were leveled once more at the pursuing infernal devices. Rockson ordered, "Open up with everything you have."

"Hold your fire," Rona said. "Try lobbing these babies." She had broken open a barrel with the butt of her rifle and found some useful items.

McCaughlin was handed one. "*Helmets!*" he exclaimed.

They had all seen the things seize the helmet that Chen had thrown at them, and had all wished they had taken one of the Death City souvenirs with them. Now they had ample supplies of the things. These were more-ordinary steel affairs—brown twentieth-century U.S. Army combat helmets. They'd do.

The Freefighters broke open more barrels and heaved away the contents. Each helmet tossed meant one less bomb. And in a matter of fifty tosses, there were no more of the little bastards to follow them.

Rockson and the others slowly rose from their positions.

Rock dropped the helmet in his hand. "There are only a handful of the helmets left. It was a good thing we ran out of scabies before we ran out of helmets."

"Now what?" Detroit asked.

"*Now we go on*," Rock said, with determination—and pain—etched in his voice. He shook away helping hands as he tore a piece of fabric from his jacket and tied up the leg wound. "It didn't hit any major vessels. I can walk — even if it smarts a bit."

Rockson hoped that the corridor would shortly bring them to the fissure that led to Eden. Instead they exited the corridor into another cavern, this one lit by some sort of luminous rock, and filled with brilliant amethyst crystal formations. "Man," said Detroit, "This is really something."

Danik exclaimed, "We are at the threshhold of Eden. In the stories — they speak of an Amethyst Cave that sends pleasant cool winds into Eden via a fissure near the lake. This is the place."

"Well, I never saw the likes of something like this," McCaughlin said. "You must be right."

Rockson told them to fan out and try to find a wind — the escaping cool air that flowed into their destination.

Archer found the draft. His big floppy hat blew off, and was almost sucked into the crevice. His beard fluttered, his crystal skull-filling flashed with red and blue sparks of excitment. "*Heeeerrreee*," he yelled.

Rock told the others to sit down a bit before they plunged into Eden. He had decided on a plan of action. A plan that all except Archer — who always agreed with Rock — and Detroit and Chen thought might work. All the others were dead set against it.

"I'll make it orders," Rock said, once he told them of his idea. "It's the only way I can imagine we can overcome all of Eden's forces in one blow."

# Chapter 22

At that very moment in Eden, in the steam room of his private rooms adjoining the austere Government Building, Stafford lounged restfully. He loved the steam, the heat, the sweating. His flaccid, hairy body responded to it, sang with the steam hissing from the heated rocks.

And he didn't like to be disturbed in these sojourns into peace. The affairs of state were most trying, and he had to have his relaxation.

The door at the far end of the misty room opened. A cool breeze came in.

"Mannerly? Is that you? Shut the damned door."

"Sir," said Mannerly, the butler, coming in quickly and closing the door, "where are you?"

"Over here. At the far end. Come over here and speak. What do you want? What's so important?"

"Sir," said the tall tuxedoed Mannerly, stepping carefully on the slick tiles, "there are visitors. Most urgent, they say."

"Urgent? Have you their card?"

"Yessir," Mannerly replied.

"Then bring it here, at once."

Mannerly managed to reach his master in a few more moments of dangerous slipping and sliding. He leaned over the seated naked man and proffered a silver tray, upon which was a single business card.

Stafford grumbled and picked it up. It was already soggy. *Bdos Err, Chief of the Civil Guard*, it said.

"Hrummph," Stafford said, "Well, I guess I must see him — fetch me that robe over there . . ."

Mannerly gingerly stepped to the hook and removed the white robe, then brought it to Stafford.

Stafford walked while he put it on, and Mannerly followed, hoping to not get lost in the steam.

Stafford, once out into the gray-carpeted gray living room bare of any decorations, sat down in his audience chair, clad in his robe. He looked up at the tall pinch-nosed Mannerly. His tuxedo was quite soggy, and damp, all the starch coming out of it. Stafford grinned. He looked positively uncomfortable. He himself was quite comfortable. The heat of the volcanic heated sauna room lingered in his bones. "Show Bdos Err in, Mannerly, don't just stand there."

Bdos Err, all six foot six, three hundred muscular pounds of him, toting his bullwhip in his hamhock-sized fist and wearing metal armor-mail, strode in noisily. At his side were his two martial arts experts, Nunchaku-man and Dedman. They wore plainer outfits, black synth-leather fighting suits.

They looked formidable, and were. In the recent disturbances, they had struck terror — and death — into the rising tide of dissenters to Stafford's iron rule.

Bdos Err was the toughest man in Eden. Stafford

wished he had more like him. The Civil Guard was too weak, too soft.

"Sir," the Guard chief began, saluting across his broad chest of steel, "our detectors buried in the floor of the Amethyst Cave show movements in the area."

"Earth tremors?"

"No sir—footsteps. We weren't sure at first, they were so far away—but they are getting louder—and a few minutes earlier, a whole series of sharp reports—explosions."

Stafford stood up and wrapped the robe's belt around his rather rotund waist. He balled his fists and hissed, "It must be Danik."

"Or an attack from Death City, sir. We've been expecting one for fifty years."

"No," said Stafford, "it's Danik. He's come back . . . How many people are there coming our way?" Stafford's forehead was a mass of wrinkles of concern.

"A half-dozen, perhaps a few more."

Stafford smiled. "That's around the same number we suspect Danik left with. So, he returns from the surface. I told him—*and* his party of fools—that the surface is impossible. A terrible unlivable hell. Well, his failure will show the people how correct I am . . . Bdos, it is good you come here with these words. I want the group rounded up the minute they exit into our paradise. I do not want either him or any of his party injured—just apprehended." Stafford smiled, pacing back and forth, thinking. "Yes, they are to be executed in the Public Square. That will end the last resistance to my rule. The dissenters figure Danik to be their leader—his death before their eyes . . ."

201

"What are my orders, sir?"

"Go to the Lake Area, keep a lookout near the crevice that leads to the caverns. Apprehend anyone who emerges. Bring them to me."

"If they resist?" These words of Bdos Err brought twisted smiles to his companions' faces, for they were adepts at rendering pain, at destroying flesh. Numchaku-man fingered the two metal sticks attached to a chain shoved into his waistband. And Dedman tightened his grip on the steel shaft of a spear that he held to his side.

"Use whatever level of violence the situation demands. No more. If you must use the disintegrators, use low power. Don't entirely burn them up. There must be enough left to torture, and to display in the Square."

Bdos Err saluted smartly, and he and his grim companions in terror exited the apartments.

Stafford was now restless. He would not return to the steam; instead he had Mannerly hand him his tunic. He put it on and went into the entertainment area.

No one in Eden lived as well as Stafford. No one had a steam bath, an entertainment area, or the other amenities. But then again, no one else had the *guts* to seize power and *take* what he wanted, Stafford mused.

He sat down in a lounge chair in the artificial wood-paneled room and pressed a button activating the wide screen. The lights, sound, and action of a Hollywood movie of the 1980s swept across the screen. *The Night of the Grizzlys*, his favorite movie began again. He had seen it 102 times.

He leaned back to watch the dangerous creatures of the surface walk again, terrorizing and tearing flesh.

To think that these creatures existed even before the nuke war. What hideous things Danik must have seen, what terror must have driven him back into the arms of his executioner now, in this age of mutations above. Yes, the surface had been dangerous even before the radiation mutated the creatures into more hellish forms. These movies proved it.

He wondered now, a look of concern crossing his face. Were those footsteps that Bdos Err had told him of *human*? Or were they . . . *monsters* from the surface world?


Rockson and his group came stumbling out of the narrow fissure into brilliant, whitish sunlight. At first Rockson thought somehow they had returned to the surface, but then he saw the reeds waving in the cool winds from the cavern behind them. They were green, and so were the lily pads, with their multicolor lotus flowers.

It was winter, and even at this latitude, the plant life was all dead on the surface. Another tipoff was the sun above—it had a paleness, an unhealthy quality, that the real sun never had. It was a lithium-boron flame. Burns for a thousand years . . . The air smelled stale and malodorous, like a closed tomb. That's what Eden was—a closed tomb.

"We must be in Eden. Pretty foul smelling." Rock stated. His eyes were adjusting to the harsh artificial sunlight. The others commented upon the foul air—and the restrained sunlight also. Rona said, "Why, if the hole into the caverns didn't exist, they would have suffocated here."

"Long as the air's breathable," Detroit said as a way of breaking through the delay, "let's get going."

Danik said, "You're right—I know the area ahead well—it's a shallow lake; we can wade along in the reeds till we reach the flowerbeds. Then we can filter into town, and contact my friends, plan our attack."

Rockson, favoring his injured leg, turned to look back where they had come out of the fissure. It was almost invisible at this angle. Just the flutter of the grass near what appeared to be a solid rock wall gave any indication of the hole. No wonder so few in Eden knew of it.

Bdos Err had kept his men quiet and low in the barge for a half hour. And his patience and stealth was rewarded. The sounds of men wading, rippling the water in the reeds not far off. He knew he had his catch. And better still, the fish were walking right into the fisherman's lap.

"Halt, and don't move for your weapons," he said, rising and pointing his disintegrator forward. His soldiers, scattered about the reeds up to their knees in the waters, did likewise. Twenty disintegrators leveled on the seven strangely garbed intruders—before they could raise their odd weapons.

The intruders, a strange lot, stood there in the waist-deep waters. Danik was among them, but these others—they were not the dissenters he had expected to catch. They were bizzarely appareled men of strong physique not unlike his own. And there was a tall

204

woman among them, a woman who put the women of Eden to shame in her strong beauty.

"Stafford's elite guard," Danik exclaimed, a note of hopelessness in his strained voice. He was soon cringing behind the Rockson. "We have come so far and now we are doomed, Rockson. Those are disintegrators they are brandishing."

"We are not dead yet," Rockson snapped, and in the Anasazi language, he muttered to Detroit Green, who stood nearest to the Doomsday Warrior, "Well that saves us the trouble of finding Stafford—as I hoped."

Detroit nodded slightly.

They made no move for their weapons. Bdos sent some men wading to disarm them while the rest kept watch, their disintegrators poised. Bdos kept a careful eye on the one with the white streak through his dark mane of hair. He stood so straight, he had *bearing*. The bearing of a warrior. He wondered if the man would surrender his odd weapon—a long-barreled ancient-style pistol. If not, Bdos Err would take the man's holster off with his bullwhip.

Once they were disarmed, the commander of the guard ordered that they be tied by their elbows, behind their backs.

While this was done, Nunchaku-man came up alongside his leader in the barge and whispered, "Are they surface people? They look somewhat like us."

"Maybe looks are deceiving," said Bdos. "Maybe they look like us but are monsters underneath." That comment brought a grin to the tall multi-scarred face next to him. "Maybe they can take more torture than our citizens—maybe they will last longer. Their eyes are strange . . . especially that one with the white streak through his hair. And that woman—have you ever seen such a tall woman—of such coloring? Maybe they are humanoid, but they are not human."

"Keep your weapons accurately aimed, men," Bdos ordered as the prisoners were helped aboard the barge.

# Chapter 23

The barge motor was turned on and the flat wide boat that had lain hidden in the reeds slowly moved out low in the water, carrying its prisoners back to Eden City. Rockson and the tall muscled bald man who was the leader of the Civil Guard, the man they called Bdos Err, had a sort of staring contest. Rockson sensed the man was not like his two henchmen. No, this Bdos Err had some sort of nobility. What was it? A sense of purpose? What purpose could an intelligent man have in serving a mad dictator? No, it wasn't purpose he saw in the burly man wearing the metal armor. It was — duty. Yes, duty propelled this man. Not avarice, or cunning, but simply duty. The perfect soldier — obeys orders. Obeys anyone in authority, even the mad. Even to commit atrocities if so ordered.

Rockson spent less time on the two henchmen. The one they called Nunchaku-man was of an estimable height, and like his boss, the man appeared well muscled and alert. But that half-grin he wore, the curl of those lips under that long twisted black moustache . . . Sadism, pure and simple. He was in his position because he was terror incarnate. Men who would not fear Bdos, despite the man's power and his blind obedience, feared the wrath of Nunchaku-man.

And at the stubby bow of the barge, his face to the warm foul wind, stood Dedman. Dedman — what an apt name for the gray-faced expressionless killer with the sword stuck jauntily into his scabbard. He held that long metal spear of his — Rock noted the bit of dried red on its tip — as if it were a part of his physique. He had a rigid posture; his eyes were like that of an automaton.

Danik whispered information about the three Civil Guards. They were raised in an abnormal way — the result of genetic experiments, they had been created *in vitro*, in petri dish fertilization. They had been kept by machines, fed intravenously for ten years, fed a special vitamin formula that made them stronger than all the others of Eden. All the others in the experiment had died but these three. They'd been taught the arts of death by an old man, the last of his warrior class, some dozen years ago.

Rockson paid scant attention to the rest of the thin crew that had disarmed and bound him and his friends. They would be nothing without their disintegrator sidearms. And probably not very good with the weapons, either. The three leaders showed their disdain for the lower ranks by not carrying any modern weapons. If there was a showdown, the coiled bullwhip of Bdos Err and the nunchaku and

208

the sword and spear of his henchmen would be the difficulty.

The water vessel approached the docks now. Before Rockson, in a chemical-brown smog of stale air, stood the oddest city Rockson had ever encountered in all his journeys. It was so damned squalid. Sooty five- or six-story buildings, totally devoid of adornment; featureless, storeless streets perfectly perpendicular to one another.

The gray-brown buildings seemed to eat up the faint artificial sunlight that poured down from above. No building, as far as Rock could see from the barge, had any design or style except the geometric — cubes, triangles, pentagons. The building blocks must have been cut from gray basalt or like volcanic rock. And built according to some simple, unimaginative, functional formula.

No, that wasn't *quite* true . . . Rockson saw, at the far side of the cavern-city about five hundred yards down the broad main avenue, a taller building. A seven-story job. The other buildings in the city had no glass; this one seemed to be made *entirely* of black glass. It glimmered bleakly in the eternal sunlight.

The broad avenue leading to it filled with activity. From the hidden side streets poured a crowd of squat, pale, listless people. They headed toward the docks, not with excitement, which would be the expected response, but with a measured, almost parade-like cadence. When they reached the concrete abutment bordering the landing area, they stood about looking at the strange doings with almost-glassed colorless eyes. Most were of the short variety, the common mold of Edenites, Rockson saw. But some were tall

209

and ungainly slender, with pink eyes like Danik's. This was a dismal group.

They were summarily unloaded, their captors herding them soundlessly up the ramp. The crowd of onlookers parted to allow them to be marched down the broad avenue toward what, Rockson supposed, was Stafford's Government Building. The edifice at the end of the avenue.

As they approached Stafford's headquarters, Rock felt that this particular building seemed to exude evil from its volcanic-glass bricks. Its stolid structure glinted ominously, absorbing and bending the unhealthy "sun's" light.

The leader of the Freefighters could see himself and the others twisting and turning grotesquely in the poorly cut glassy stone walls of the building. They were paraded around to the rear, and up to the wide staircase entrance. The stairs were high, and entered the building halfway up. An odd thing, Rockson thought. Perhaps it was done to intimidate. This structure *was* intimidating.

They were urged along with the disintegrators at their backs, told to ascend the long staircase. Each Freefighter had his own guard holding him.

There was no bannister, and by the time one reached the open doorway it was a bone-breaking drop on both sides of the stairs. Rockson considered that he could easily shove his particular guard off the precipitous topmost step and manage to land upon him, but what would that avail him? More Civil Guards stood below with their disintegrators leveled. The city was an armed camp. No, best to wait — for a better time to make a move. Though he didn't know how he would manage, with the elbows-together, awkward way he was bound. It hurt. His circulation was being cut off. Plus, he still favored one leg.

Into the circular chamber of the black cube building strode the captors and their charges. A crowd of gray-robed short men — dressed somewhat, Rockson thought, like Roman senators — were milling about the large chamber. They noted the new arrivals well, and then reset their eyes upon the center of the room.

Bdos Err pushed himself through the crowd of "senators," who were truly eager to give the metal-wearing giant the right of way.

The milling robed crowd became hushed. Rockson could see the man seated in a black onyx glass chair at the center of the room now. Stafford. He wore a big gray-jewel ring on each of his fat fingers, his hair was short and sparse and combed forward — a bit like Nero. He was flabby under that blue tunic, Rockson guessed. At first Rockson thought he was old, but then he realized it was just the thinning hair color and his grayish pallor. The man could be just in his thirties, judging by the smooth skin of his flaccid, unwrinkled face. An unhealthy man. And sick men in power do sick things. His gray eyes were unfocused.

"Sir," Bdos Err reported, saluting smartly, his left hand crossing his chest of metal. "We have apprehended Danik's party as they came into our paradise."

Stafford smiled, "Wonderful. Wonderful. Bring them forth."

Bdos snapped out rapid orders, and the Freefighters, with Danik in front, were brought before the chair and lined up so that Stafford could view them.

211

"What's this? Stafford said, rising from his black chair in surprise. "Who are these people? They are most strange . . ." He rubbed his chin, stepping over to Danik. Stafford put his face near the tall albino and said, "Danik, what manner of beings have you brought back with you from the surface? Some sort of radiation mutations, no doubt. Eh?"

"These are my friends," Danik said. "And they are proof that the surface world is livable. And not only livable, a paradise of light and color and fresh air."

"*Heresy,*" someone muttered, and then a chant went up among the senators, "Heresy, heresy, heresy . . ."

Stafford waved his hand in the air, and the chant subsided.

"Well, well. Friends, you say? Let me look these odd mutants over for a moment." Stafford walked slowly down the line as if he were reviewing an honor guard, as if he were going to say, "Tighten that collar, mister; straighten your posture, recruit."

But he paused an extra long time when he reached Rona. He looked her up and down. Not with sexual desire, but with curiosity.

"A woman of the surface? Indeed, she is too well built for a woman. She is definitely a mutant."

Then Stafford came to Rockson. "Mismatched eyes, huh," Stafford commented. "And a white streak in your hair. My my, another mutant." He lifted his flaccid many-ringed hand and pressed a finger to Rockson's chin. Rockson twisted his face to the side. Stafford smiled. "And a spunky mutant at that, eh?"

Stafford went to his chair, and climbed up on one broad flat arm of it. "Edenites," Stafford shouted, his voice echoing in the chamber, "Danik has returned and brought us some curious surface dwellers. What shall we do with the traitor and his friends from the dark realms above?"

"Kill . . . torture . . . burn . . ." came the assortment of replies from the floor.

The situation didn't look good.

# Chapter 24

Stafford waved his hand for the assemblage to be quiet. "In a while. In a while . . ." he promised.

Stafford walked back down the line to Danik.

"Why so dour," Stafford taunted, "on such a joyous occasion? By the way, what happened to Run Dutil and the others of your traitorous party?"

"They perished, but not because of radiation or mutant animals attacking. But because we, as underground dwellers all our lives, were unprepared for the vast distances, the cold temperatures of this season. They perished from exhaustion, exposure, lack of food. All of this is no reason to remain underground here in this tomb you so ironically call a *paradise.*"

"Perished, huh," Stafford said. "Well, I told you, I told *all* the dissenters, that the surface was dangerous. Now the remaining dissenters will give up their mad desires to reach the outer world."

Danik shouted, "*No,* you must not heed this madman. Stafford is wrong, dead wrong. The surface isn't as he says. Sure, it is dangerous — but only because we don't know how to deal with it. But we can learn, learn from the great Americans who live and fight and triumph up there in God's nature. You should see it, you should *feel* it. I was hungry, and cold, and

215

tired, and I fully expected to die—and so did the others. Yet not one of us, once we had been outside for more than a few minutes, once we had seen the sunrise, the clouds, once we had smelled God's good air, tasted fresh water and drank of the infinitely good sunlight, would have ever returned to our dismal lives here. Eden is not beautiful, not a paradise; it is a drab *hell*."

Stafford yawned. "This is tiring, really, Danik." He went to sit down on his black throne. Evidently, Rockson noted, a bit of walking is all the man can endure as exercise. He's even in worse shape than I imagined.

Stafford opened up a compartment in the arm of the chair and extracted a sharp instrument. He started picking at his manicured nails. The epitome of cool, that's what he wants to appear before his minions, Rock knew. He had seen that act before, that posed nonchalance. All the sick leaders of the world wanted to appear above it all.

"Ah yes, the surface has its dangers," Stafford muttered, smiling up at Bdos Err, who stood at rigid attention to his right. "Why leave paradise? I told them—but they wouldn't listen. I only want to save my people from death, and the likes of Danik tries to lead them to it." He pointed to Danik with the nail file. "Well now, Danik, you know the penalty for treason. So what I do with *you* is simple. But what about these others? What do I do with this bearded monster with the crystals growing out of his head? What do I do with the one with the white streak in his hair, the masculine woman, the others from the surface hell?"

216

Rockson spoke up, having observed Stafford's behavior for a sufficient time to develop a psychological strategy.

Rockson now saw that there was no talking to the little man-who-would-be-God. His megalomania allowed no rational discourse. And with that realization, Rockson developed another strategy. The man was proud, vain. A little god. And with such men, there was only one course, until you could overpower them through cunning. Rockson would *play up to Stafford*. He would feed the man's ego.

"I am the leader of my group," said Rockson, "I am a mutant, that is true, but I can appreciate true leadership and knowledge. I never dreamed that Eden could be so beautiful and clean. Had I known what wonders there were here, I would never have believed Danik's madness. This is paradise. The surface is hell. If I die, I will die happy to have seen the beauty here, happy to have witnessed true leadership."

Stafford eyed him up and down, and finally said, "You are wiser than you look. Though you are a mutation, I might have a use for you — but not for the others . . ."

Stafford ordered the rest of the Freefighters and Danik held in the detention cells until suitable arrangements for their public humiliation and then execution could commence.

And Stafford ordered the senators to leave also. He told Bdos and his two henchmen and a contingent of six guards to remain behind. And bade Rockson stay and talk for a while.

Once the prisoners had been escorted from the chamber, and the senators, gossiping and gesturing to one another, had left, Stafford clapped his hands and said, "Mannerly, have the doctor come and treat our friend's leg—it obviously needs help."

The servant returned with a squat silent man, who opened a bag and took out some salve that he applied to Rock's wound. It worked wonders.

Rockson sat, tasting hors d'oeuvres and what looked like cheese but tasted like shit from the tray Mannerly brought. He took a little wine, which wasn't as bad, because he was thirsty.

Pouring on the flattery, Rock ingratiated himself to the dictator for more than an hour. Finally, Stafford said, "Perhaps you would like to see more of our wondrous city."

"I would be honored," Rockson replied. Now this was more like it. Perhaps he could find some way out—maybe if they got careless he could still instigate his original plan. Seize Stafford, and order the patrols to lay down their arms.

But Stafford was a cunning sort, well used to intrigues and treachery. When he and the Doomsday Warrior set out on their brief tour of Eden, they were accompanied by ten guards. And Rockson was not unbound. However, his elbow bindings were removed to make him more comfortable, though his wrists were still held in check behind his waist. Ah well, some progress is better than no progress.

The two-bit "king" started pointing out the "grand" sites.

Always the watchful phalanx of Civil Guards with drawn weapons kept a close eye on them.

"First, Rockson, I will show you the new sources of food. I realized that we were exhausting the canned

218

and preserved foods provided in abundance over a hundred years ago. I have instituted bold new measures to produce more food. We do not need the poisonous surface soil to raise food."

"What is your new means of production, King Charles? Is it hydroponic gardening? If you intend to do that you need grow lights. Your sun is not sufficiently full-spectrum." Rockson stopped and smiled broadly. "Of course, I am being foolish. You have some completely new revolutionary method of food production in mind. Am I right?"

"Yes," the king said. "We will have no need for water and minerals and grow lights. There is an easier way than hydroponics . . . Come along, I will show you."

Soon they had passed through a blasted-away rock wall into the most foul-smelling place Rockson had ever encountered. Machines similar to big Soviet bulldozers were moving around piles of fecal matter and garbage. The air—if it could be called that—was filled with little gnats that insisted on buzzing his face. What was all this mad activity about? The cacophony of grinding gears, the smell of the fecal rot, was hardly endurable to the Doomsday Warrior. But evidently the Edenites, including the king, had less sensitive sensory apparatus.

The King boasted, "Here, the fecal waste of four generations of Eden has lay wasted. We are in the so-called 'disposal cave,' " Stafford said. "This precious resource has been lying here sealed off, wasted.

"I have decided to use this precious resource. The excretions of the past can be processed into tasty replicas of all the necessary proteins, minerals, and fiber necessary to the human body. It can be shaped by machinery into what appears to be steaks, potatoes, and such. Coloring can be added. People would hardly know the difference. I venture to say that they *won't* know the difference between this new food supply and their old canned and preserved real foods."

In his wildest nightmare Rockson couldn't imagine this . . . People would be forced to eat— "Shit," Rockson blurted out.

"What?" asked Stafford.

"I said I am awed. This is very interesting." Rockson tried to turn his attention from the bulldozers moving the excrement piles to the metal hoppers, where a conveyor belt carried the matter through a wall—presumably a processing plant lay beyond that wall.

The flies were getting to him; he wanted to leave. But Stafford wanted Rock's attention on a set of fifty long slender poles hanging from high above. "Note that the flies are congregating, swarming around the poles?"

"Yes," Rockson said, brushing at his face, trying to keep the little gnats from his eyes at least. Indeed the flies were droning around the many hanging poles. The poles seemed to have a sticky surface on them. Flies were massed in some places inches deep on the stickiness.

"I see you're trying to do something about the fly problem," Rockson said, not knowing what was expected of him.

"*Do* something about them?" the king said, as if incredulous at the stupidity of the comment. "My

220

dear fellow, we are *collecting them,* they will be the source of the *flavoring* of the new food."

Rockson was happy he had a strong stomach. Still, the remark was almost too much. He watched in mute horror as special "skimming" vehicles crawled up to the most fly-clogged poles and a cylindrical device slid up over the poles and sucked off the dead flies. The trucks, once this was accomplished, deposited their flies in a hopper next to the fecal conveyor belts.

"See," bragged the king, "we have no need of returning to the surface to make food. With these innovations, we will have enough food forever."

"Fascinating, King Charles . . ." muttered the Freefighter. "Now, could we perhaps see that park you mentioned? The one that doesn't need maintenance?"

"Yes, yes, of course," the king said. They exited the abominable scene, and Rockson was never so glad to leave a place in his life.

The "park," which was two blocks from the fecal cavern, consisted of thirty brown-metal poles painted with barklike graphics. They were supposed to be the maintenance-free trees of Eden. Rockson leaned against one. It was cold and steely to the touch. The grass below their feet was the kind of matting they'd used to use in football stadiums — when the pollution of the 1980s made it impossible to maintain real grass fields.

Several backless benches in the park, among the evenly distributed "trees," were occupied by oldsters. The withered men and women, sacklike forms that drooled out on their tunics, were watching a group of

221

painters repaint a peeling "tree."

"Nice park," Rockson said. "I don't see any children playing, though."

"We have—reproductive problems," Stafford admitted begrudgingly. "It's our one negative. But I have teams of my best scientists working on the problem. Years ago we had some experiments in genetics that resulted in the three strong leaders of the Guard. I am hoping to reproduce those successes without the necessity of sexual intercourse, which is, of course, a filthy animal practice."

"Of course," Rockson agreed. What else could he say? "Well, it's a very nice park . . ." Rockson glanced up—the homogenously green painted boughs above had no individual leaves, just a mottled texture created by paint brushes. "I see there's no troublesome leaves to rake up in the fall."

"Leaves? Fall?"

"On the surface, parts of the trees—er—peel off at a certain time each year, and have to be raked up."

"We don't have any such problems in Eden."

Onward they walked. Rockson never had a chance to seize a weapon from the eternally watchful guards.

The king was tired, though the tour was less than a half-hour old.

They went back to the Government Building.

Stafford said, "Rockson, I have decided not to kill you surface people. You will be exhibited. I fancy that I will create a zoo. Danik will die, of course, and most painfully and publicly. You and your company of freaks will be well fed, with the best of the new food."

"That is kind of you."

222

"It is not kindness. The one thing that Danik has said that seemed to be right is the fact that our genes *have* suffered somehow from being underground. Sex is a dirty and primitive thing, but the race must go on. The need for fresh genetic material is obvious, and you surface men — and that buxom surface woman — must have some potency. I will let my scientists use you for experiments. To our genetic problems, you surface beings present a possible solution both simple and practical.

"I am not unfamiliar with the sciences. Do you realize that a single fertile woman of the past — who was, I suppose, of the type similar to the redhead surface woman — could produce ten, twenty ova a month? If removed surgically, each ova could be implanted in our barren women and fertilized by inserting genetic material derived from you surface men."

It was all Rockson could do to contain himself. Zoo exhibits, specimens for experiments, horrible operations on Rona — there wasn't much time to act. He didn't relish being a farm for genes to keep propagating these mole people. And Rockson gagged at the thought of Rona being a "donor," confined to a hospital bed, constantly operated upon for removal of human egg cells. He nodded, though, as if it were a good deal, to eat all that great shit-food, to be alive.

# Chapter 25

The king excused himself to "tend to his toilet." He ordered that Rockson be unbound and treated to some food and drink while he "freshened up."

This was more like it, Rock thought. His easy acquiescence to the abominable ideas of this madman finally had paid off. Rockson, unbound, rubbed his sorely aching wrists. He didn't want to drink or eat anything offered to him, though he was powerfully hungry. The thought of the way they were making food here in this underground madhouse stayed his hunger.

He sat for five minutes in the second chair in the audience room, but Stafford did not return. Instead Mannerly, the butler in the tux, came in and said, "The king wishes you to come to his study, for further conversation in a more comfortable environment."

The study, attached directly to the throne chamber, turned out to be an antiseptically bare room with computer disk cases lining the walls. Only two guards were left there to watch Rockson, apparently on the king's order.

Rockson had been looking around everywhere he had been taken for a sign of the old steel safe that Danik believed would be the location of the dreaded

Factor Q germ-warfare canister. Rockson's intense eyes perused the study, its shelves of computer disk boxes, its plain metal cabinets and—

A bolt of adrenaline shot into his system, for in the corner of the study was a safe. An ancient type, with a combination lock. Could it be?—*yes.*

There was a warning painted on it. *Caution. Do not approach safe. Automatic countermeasures fatal to humans are activated unless verbal disarm code is given.*

He smiled. The Doomsday Warrior knew what to do now, and if he was right, the code would be no problem. The king would supply it.

He calmed himself, readied his well-muscled frame to respond instantly when the moment was most conducive to success. There might never be another chance like this. His plan, the one Danik thought to be sheer madness, had carried him to this juncture— to a position that all the fighting in the world would not have accomplished. Here he sat in the recesses of the Government Building's inner private room, inches away from his goal. Surrender as a way of attack. Only Chen understood the concept. Only Chen approved of this daring gamble. And now, it was close to paying off . . .

Seconds counted. Where was the king? Rockson was sure that if Bdos Err came upon him sitting with only two soldiers guarding, he would immediately increase security. And the chance would slip away, forever.

He waited for what seemed like eons.

Finally, Stafford entered through the guarded portal and smiled. He wore a new greenish tunic, and his thin hair was combed back. He looked refreshed.

Rockson stood up and made to go over and shake his hand, or something, saying with a broad grin, "Man, you have a fabulous—" Then the Doomsday Warrior, moving like a flash, grabbed Stafford's arm. He wrenched it behind him, put him into a hammerhold. "One move for your weapons and I snap the king's neck," he snarled.

The hapless Civil Guards, momentarily confused, turned their guns upon Mannerly, the manservant, who had just entered holding a tray of hors d'oeuvres. He fell with an agonized expression, his tux burned away to a depth of six inches, his midsection cremated by the twin beams of the disintegrator pistols.

"Drop the weapons," Rock said, making to strangle the king.

"Please, please drop the weapons . . ." said the helpless man Rock held in a mighty grip.

The soldiers' weapons clattered to the floor. They were both staring at the smoking corpse of the butler with something like guilt on their stupid faces.

Rockson twisted Stafford's flaccid countenance half around, and demanded, "The code to deactivate the safe's destruct mode—and then the combination. Quickly; *tell me or die*."

"I—I don't know it—I—"

"He doesn't know it," said a familiar voice from the portal. Rock looked over to see Stafford—another Stafford—standing there with three more soldiers, and with Bdos towering behind him. "He doesn't know it because you are holding a double. I am the real Stafford. I never returned after I went to freshen

227

up—instead my double was sent in. I have seen too much treachery in my magnificent life to be fooled, to be suckered."

Rockson played it out—he might just be really holding the correct man. Maybe the man in the doorway was the double.

"I warn you, I will snap his neck if—"

Bdos Err stepped forward, and, taking one of the disintegrators from a soldier, leveled it at the man who Rock held so tightly and shot him. It was a narrow beam of energy, aimed accurately directly at the man's chest. It burned a hole six inches deep. The man gagged, and his eyes rolled up. He slumped in Rockson's grip, and steaming blood and chunks of flesh-matter came bubbling out of his lips.

Rockson sighed mightily, and dropped the body.

"Now," snarled Bdos, "you know which is which."

"I use a double on many occasions," the real Stafford smirked out. "And there a dozen more where that one came from. I don't like falsehood. I don't like *false* friends. You will be treated to the same fate that the others will have. And I have decided—there will be no delay in your deaths. You are too dangerous. Too damned dangerous and cunning.

"I have decided that the surface is even more dangerous a place than I imagined. I planned to send the probe up to the surface at some future date. The probe with the Factor Q canister in it, set to burst when it reaches the surface. Now I will accelerate the completion of the probe shaft. The release of Factor Q will take place as soon as possible, in a matter of hours.

"I will eliminate the life-forms above—all humans

and animals. There will be no threat from above, and the few dissenters will cease their clamoring to be allowed to leave Eden. *There will be no habitable place on Earth except Eden.*

Deep in the dungeon beneath the Government Building, a bloodied Rockson, thrown in with his companions, told his tale of almost-success.

"You tried," Detroit comforted. "You tried and almost succeeded. It just wasn't in the cards."

Chen patted him on the shoulder. "We'll get another chance. You have mutant's luck, remember?"

Rockson tried to smile. He didn't feel very lucky. He buried his head in his hands and slumped on the cold iron bench.

In a short while the cell door clanked open, and under heavy guard, the Freefighters and Danik, all of whom were not only chained elbows-behind-the-back, but also with ankle chains that made any long strides impossible, were ushered out to the streets of Eden.

There was a timelessness about the place. It was still broad daylight. It was always broad daylight in Eden.

They were all force-marched to the west edge of Eden City. The populace, gathered to watch their traverse, were encouraged to scourge them, and scourge them they did. Rocks, whipcords, feces, bombarded the prisoners. Finally, they reached the dome that Rockson immediately knew was that of a planetarium.

He didn't get it. Not until Stafford came along and

told them, with a sly hidden meaning lingering in his words, that "certain modifications," had been carried out on the planetarium. The king said, "Enjoy the show," and left.

They were pushed and kicked, forced inside the door of the building.

They were strapped into the theaterlike seats, in the first row of the slanting auditorium, just in front of the darkened praying-mantis-shaped sky projector.

Once secured, they were left. The doors were shut and they were immersed in total darkness. Then slowly the stars came out. A beautiful night. Clear, and bright. All the constellations, all the stars of the universe appeared, the planetarium's huge projector moving and whirring to produce the beautiful effect.

It seemed harmless. Beautiful, as a matter of fact. But Rockson's mutant instinct sensed death — imminent death. How it would come, what form it would take, he didn't know.

But he knew they were about to die — and painfully.

# Chapter 26

"Quickly, everyone — we must free ourselves. Spare no effort," Rockson implored.

The Freefighters had seldom heard that tone of voice in their leader, and they immediately complied. Of all of them, Rona had the best chance of success. She had been, as a teenager, a roving circus performer, an acrobat with the entire Wallender family. The family had toured Red-held America, putting on shows and secretly gathering intelligence for the Freefighter cause. She was a contortionist, and the skill had served her well in the past.

But these were no ordinary shackles that could be removed by forcing a shoulder out of socket, or by any such maneuvers.

The sky began a subtle change. They *appeared* to be in a rocket, the planets slipping slowly by. The journey started out by ringed green Neptune and its companion moons. Then they slid majestically past

Uranus, seventh planet, the one with its axis tilted completely askew to its orbit about the Sun.

*The Sun.* The word set off something in Rockson's sixth sense. Something about the Sun . . .

And he gasped. He knew what Stafford had in mind, he knew what the modifications done to the planetarium were for.

*They were in a crematorium.*

Jupiter slid by; the orange globe spun serenely, the shadows of its dozen-plus moons moving across its turbulent lines of methane and ammonia clouds. The huge Red Spot came into view, the eternal megahurricane of its equatorial regions.

They didn't have much time left. Far off in the distance, a dim star—Sol, the earth's sun—was getting brighter. They were plunging faster now, and faster, the gravity of the 865,000-mile-wide star that warmed all the planets of the solar system becoming a disk. A hot yellow disk.

Mars and its irregular-shaped moons, the cratered lumpy Phobos and Deimos, slid by silently. The planetarium was no longer cool. Slowly, ever so slowly, the temperature had risen. And that was only the beginning.

It was hard to ignore the beautiful space vista on the dome and concentrate on all one's might, all one's will, on the bindings that held them in the death building.

Earth loomed up; they passed the Moon, the beautiful companion world to the blue and white planet. The wrecked, abandoned space platforms of the Soviet Union and the United States swept by in a flash. The bodies of astronauts and cosmonauts eternally preserved in their punctured, scarred space-suits flickered in the imagination.

It grew hotter. The others had now guessed what Rockson hadn't expressed to them. They all knew that the imaginary journey through the solar system was not just a visual experience. They knew that the place was rigged to give the *heat* effect of their destination—*the sun itself*.

"I'm making progress," Rona shouted. "Just . . . a . . . little more . . . " She had painfully dislocated both her shoulders; he agony-wracked body was now able to slip down under the steel belt that held it in place on the death seat.

"I'm out," she said, and there were snapping noises and a terrible groan. She had refixed her shoulders in place. She hobbled along, still in her ankle chains, to the Doomsday Warrior.

Venus, the planet named after the Goddess of Love herself, slipped rapturously by the unwilling voyagers. The heat of the burning, glaring disk of the Sun now was unbearable, but was briefly eclipsed by the crescent orb.

"The projector, smash the projector," Rock yelled.

Rona jumped up and started beating on the metal monster with her fists, then kicked it with her best shot. Nothing. The show went on. She found some blinking lights and a panel—the controls. She bootheeled them with a vicious series of downward kicks. No result.

Rockson had the impression that they couldn't be broken. He shouted, "Tear a leg loose from that steel lectern table, Rona. Use it to pry my seat out of the damned floor. It's bolted in."

She accomplished bashing a leg of the table loose and had started applying it as a pry-bar under Rockson when the Sun came out of eclipse. The planet of love sailed by, no longer able to stop the heat from rising again.

It must have been a hundred and twenty degrees fahrenheit by the time Rona had half pried Rock's chair from its concrete base. And it was far too late now for any one of them to survive.

Rockson, sweat pouring down his forehead, watched as the cratered lead-rivered planet Mercury appeared. The closest planet to the Sun. The Sun was the size of a giant fireball, too brilliant to look at even for an instant. The heat was near the point that they would collapse and die, screaming their lungs out in final pain.

It was over. The fight was over. They were as good as dead.

The sky suddenly went utterly black. There was a hiss — some hidden air conditioner came on. The temperature rapidly dropped to normal levels.

The plunge into the inferno of the Sun had only been a teaser. The main event was now coming up. Twilight, artificial twilight, was falling. The stars started appearing again. The Big Dipper, the pole star, the other constellations. The stars started slowly wheeling up from the imaginary eastern horizion.

There didn't seem to be anything dangerous . . . Then it happened. The red star Antares rose, the jewel of the southern constellation of Scorpio. Antares's light seemed to intensify; there was the smell of ozone in the air.

Rockson's eyes widened in horror as he saw a stream of laser-red light shoot out from the star and start tracking across the round room, searing a smoking line of white-hot destruction in the empty seats it was traversing. The star-beam kept moving; the stream of laser death was heading his way.

Just as the ray of death reached him, Rona had wrenched his seat free. Rockson turned it on its side, placing himself under the laser beam from Antares. Rona jumped aside just in time also.

The seat behind where Rock had just been was seared in half as if a blowtorch had been applied to it.

Mightily Rockson struggled with his bindings, smashing his awkwardly immobilized body again and again against the other bolted-down seats. At last the sturdy metal of the chair gave way to the immense power of the Warrior from the Surface, and he shook off the pieces and together with Rona started making the rounds of the other Freefighters, managing to free most of them before the star, which had set for a brief time, rose again in the "southeast."

Again the false Antares started its randomly programmed death-ray crisscross of the seats. Backs of chairs, seared in half, flopped to the floor smoking hot.

It got worse. A second and a third star, blue-white Sirius and flickering Vega, also started sending out the concentrated thin beams of laser heat. The crisscrossing beams were sure to hit one of them. Those that had been helped free valiantly risked their own lives to unbind their companions, ignoring the personal danger.

McCaughlin and Archer didn't need any help tearing their chairs out of the floor once that strategy was broached to them. And they straightened up and their massive thighs and rippling sinews broke their perches to fragments. Archer even succeeded in jerking his wrists so violently that the chains holding them tore open.

"Hit the floor, keep under the cover of the chairs, and work yourselves up the aisles to the door," Rock ordered.

Rockson realized that there was a way to quickly remove the encumbering chains on their ankles and wrists. But it was an insanely desperate way. Still, if they were careful, and quick . . .

"Freefighters, hold up your chains as accurately as you can figure when the beams of light sweep by. The laser can free us as well as kill."

To demonstrate, Rockson observed the killing beam of Vega as it slid hissing across the third row. He rushed over and held his chain at a precise position—he hoped—*success*! The chain was so hot from transmitted heat that he winced in pain, but it was severed. The dangling pieces were not a real problem, the important thing was he could use his hands unencumbered.

Chen tried it next, and then the others. In a short while, with a lot of skill and luck, they had managed to unshackle themselves.

In every scene of horror there is a comedic element. Archer looked like a big rolling grizzly as he fell to the floor and lifted his legs wide to the cutting heat of a beam from Sirius. He succeeded nicely. The big mountain man was more dexterous—when he had to be—than he looked.

Rockson thought that they had all had succeeded in cutting their chains without casualty. Then there was a cry of agony. Danik had been clipped by the beam of death as he did his chains free. "I — I'm okay," he winced.

"Good man," Rock said, and he meant it. Danik was shaping up. He was no longer a wimpy, fearful mole of a man. He was one of them. Rock told him as much, and Danik smiled in the flickering death light. "Thank you."

Chen crawled over and ministered some salve to the burned-off inch of Danik's shoulder. And applied the Plasti-seal, Century City's combined antiseptic and healing bandage, that he had secreted.

Rockson believed that once the deadly star-beams had crossed every chair in the auditorium, the rays would cease. And he was correct. The stars stayed on, however, and they were able to see by their combined light. See enough to make their way to the door they had entered by.

There was no handle, and there was no seam wide enough to even get the thin blade of Rock's balisong knife into. But there was a code-punch panel, the kind that requires a numerical code in order to make the door open.

The punch-code control was hexagonal, made of cold steel. In the artificial starlight Rockson's keen mutant eyes noted that there were buttons at each corner of the metal hexagon. And one button in the middle. He read the sign next to the device.

*Open door by punching in the smaller magic number in the center and then punch in the appropriate numbers 1 through 13 on each of the points of the hexagon. Reading across each line adds up to the larger sacred number. CAUTION, improper numbers will result in activation of the planetarium's cremation cycle and the planetarium will be heated to a temperature of 451 degrees within ten seconds.*

Rockson frowned. "Any ideas, gang? Danik, you should know. You live here."

Danik flustered, "But—but each of us has our life-specialty. We do not study Liberal Arts—we do not have the well-rounded curriculum that you free men have. I am a waterworks engineer. Aside from nursery school, all my education has been about engineering. No magic numbers. That is a historian's knowledge. Stafford is a historian. I've not heard of sacred numbers, not once in all my life in Eden."

"Chen," Rock whispered, "have any idea how to solve this thing."

"Well, there were some things I studied about magic squares in ancient China. The ancients were fond of mathematical puzzles. But they are all based upon a set of sacred concepts. The concept is the key. Unless we know the concept behind the code, we can't chance a try."

"Everyone *think*. I've got to be sure of the numbers, or we will be burned alive."

"I don't know much math—but I think I've got the concept," said Rona. "I've been fascinated by dismal Eden City—no friezes, no borders, ledges, parapets, nothing in the way of adornment on any of the architecture. And there is only one geometric shape aside from the cube. That shape is the seven-sided polygon. I think the smaller magic number might be seven. I counted the steps from the dock to the shore.

238

Seven. And the steps from the ground to the entrance to Government Building is twenty-one. Try seven as the central magic number and twenty-one as the number that is the total of each line. Punch in seven in the middle, and starting at the top corner of the septagon—that's a seven-sided polygon—try thirteen, then six then eleven, then one, then eight, then three. Of course, the numbers around the edge could be different—they just have to add up to twenty-one."

"My God, how do you know this, Rona . . ."

"It isn't mystically arrived it. I noticed the number of steps in the city, and the shapes of the few buildings that weren't cubical. And I asked a guard about it—down in the dungeon. He was playing with a kind of Rubik's cube with seven sides. It had the same puzzle about 'magic numbers,' and—"

"Never underestimate a woman," McCaughlin said admiringly. "Heaven preserve you, fair Rona. You are the best."

Rockson sighed heavily. "Here goes . . ." He punched in Rona's numbers. Then he pushed the red button.

The door swung slowly open. Artificial daylight flooded into their would-be tomb.

They were free.


They cautiously ran the distance to the next building, one at a time. The streets were deserted. "It must be the sleep hours," Danik said. "I'm tired. We all get tired at the same time . . ."

There was the sound of approaching footfalls. Rockson and the others pressed close to the building wall.

A startled pair of lower-rank Civil Guards rounded the corner. They saw the Freefighters too late. They were beset immediately, and died with startled expressions, their heat guns still in their holsters.

"I would prefer my Liberator," McCaughlin said as the Freefighters made their way through the streets of Eden, startling the few timid passersby with their presence. He was holding one of the paper-light heat guns that the Edenites called disintegrators. Rona had the other one.

"We'll get our weapons back," Rona promised. "They're all piled up in a side room to Stafford's throne chamber. I saw them cart the whole pile in there and just toss them on the floor. They don't really know what to make of them, I suppose . . ."

The group of determined Americans reached the corner just across from the Government Building. Rockson had wondered what the effective range of a heat gun was, and now was the time to find out. He peered around a corner. There were two guards, one on either side of the open doorway.

Rona touched Rock's shoulder. "Let me and McCaughlin do the honors . . ."

Rock stared for a second into those determined green eyes. Then he said, "Okay, see if you can hit them with those pop-shooters, but get as close as you can without them noticing before firing."

Rona and McCaughlin just walked across the empty street and sauntered toward the entrance stairs.

The guards were facing one another, their mouths moving. Idle chatter. The last remarks they would ever make in this world.

They turned when the pair of Freefighters were a

quarter of the way up the stairs, and they died as they raised their weapons. Burned where they stood. Blackened and smoking human charcoal, they fell apart as they fell.

The rest of the Freefighters ran across the street, hardly containing a rousing cheer. One of the guard's guns had fallen; heat-damaged, it sat there on the topmost step. Rock picked it up. Useless. They walked down the corridor, and into the circular throne room.

"It's empty," Rona exclaimed.

"Perhaps they are all asleep," Danik said.

"Stafford's private apartments are to the left," Rockson stated in a low voice. "In any case, the study contains the safe. The place Stafford keeps Factor Q."

Rock ordered the rest of the Freefighters to secure the building while he plunged into Stafford's quarters.

Through the unlocked door and down the short corridor he ran, gun thrust ahead of him. Perhaps the real Stafford would be in there in his pj's. Rock could try again to force the code to open the safe from Stafford. The *real* Stafford. Awaken him from his beauty sleep with the point of the heat gun pressed against his fat face.

Happily, Rockson came upon one of the Freefighters' weapons—a baton—lying on the floor in a corner. He wondered if a soldier had pilfered it, played with it a while, then discarded it. He probably thought it just a heavy metal stick. Unless you activated the baton by pressing a certain area of the instrument, it didn't do its thing.

Rock, happy for any slight improvement in the

situation, picked it up. He had another weapon too—the one he'd taped to his body just before they entered Eden. The butterfly knife tucked on the inner thigh of his left leg. The slender blade, folded into its own handle hadn't been discovered in their cursory frisk by the inhibited guardsmen.

# Chapter 27

A steel door was shutting, a foot-thick blast-resistant door that was going to close off the room that had the safe in it. There was just a second to make it through. Rockson dived between the sliding-together masses of metal death, and rolled into the study. The twin walls of crushing steel slammed together a fraction too late to crush his feet. He had made it in.

It was utterly dark, and he had no light. Windowless buildings had that problem. He somehow thought it might not be a good idea to feel around for a light switch. Especially when he heard the muffled whispers somewhere in the room.

He eased forward in the utter darkness, trying to sense the source of those utterances. Rock snapped open his balisong knife.

A hissing sound and a red glow erupted in the far darkness. Rockson jumped to the left. The disintegrators took a fraction of a second to warm up before their heat beam shot forward—long enough for steeled reflexes to respond to the danger. The beam of intense heat burned the wall next to him. Then there was a click. The weapon had misfired, or run out of whatever juice it needed to spray hot death.

Then there was an awful silence. He lay flat, breathing through his teeth, trying to make no noise. He was blind, but the protectors of Stafford's inner sanctum couldn't see him, either. Perhaps they thought they had hit him, and were waiting for a movement, a sound, to prove otherwise. Well, he was not going to make that sound.

He slipped the balisong knife into his belt, felt for the explosive-bolt baton on his belt, slipped it into his grip. All silently. But after a minute, they won the waiting game. He didn't have time to wait any longer. He got into a crouch and moved forward, trying to remember where the furnishings were in this dark room.

Voices. Something about "I'm sure I got him. Switch on the lights."

Rock smiled, and froze in place. He was just a dozen feet from the voice, he could make it there in the dark . . .

He threw himself forward, swinging the deadly baton in an arc, intending to smash anything it encountered, and hit the soft Morris chair, not a man. He knew it the minute the baton demolished the plastic-and-fiber affair. And the lights came on, blinding. He spun and dove behind a cabinet. He peered over it.

There stood Bdos and his two henchmen, the martial arts masters known as Nunchaku-man and Dedman. Bbos held his familiar bullwhip in his left hand, coiling it tighter. Nunchaku-man took the twin sticks of death from his waistband and smiled a toothsome grin of evil. Dedman's implacable huge

244

face was enigmatic as he stood like a straight robot, holding his spear in the left hand, his other hand on the handle of his sword.

"We will see if you are as powerful a fighter as I suspect by your courage, Rockson. We will test you one at a time. Each one a fair fight. Prepare to die, intruder from the dark realm."

Nunchaku-man stepped forward, the first of the movements that would come to render him dead. The man slowly began to circle to the left. Rockson kept his distance. The man took out his two sticks of steel linked by a chain. He was starting to swing it over his head. An opening move, tentative. Nunchaku against baton and balisong knife. Well, so be it. The huge man didn't know Rock had the knife. It wasn't very obvious, tucked into his waistband. It would be his little suprise.

The knife was a versatile instrument of death. And the bolt-baton was not without its own virtues. Reach was not a virtue of either, though. Rockson had to get Nunchaku-man to move in close, or get handily defeated.

Rockson had trained in the use of the baton for many months in Century City. It was one of the standard martial arts weapons most Freefighters carried. But he'd never faced a man with skill in nunchaku manipulation with the baton. The balisong, he had used in mock combat against multiple "attackers" in the Century City gym. Just a test of skill, a feat that showed the potential of the weapon. Now he was in real combat, against three attackers. He doubted the other two, hanging back now, wouldn't join in if they could help their monstrous buddy.

A baton and a balisong against nunchaku, sword, spear, and bullwhip. One man against three towering sadistic genetic monsters.

"Piggy-face want some action?" taunted the intruder-from-the-surface. "Or is Piggy-face man afraid of me?" Rockson thought the taunt too simple, but Nunchaku-man responded with anger. And anger makes one too impulsive. The worst thing to be in a fight to the death.

Rockson let his attacker make the first move. The snarling mass of exomorphic madness stepped into Rockson's defensive circle. He held the nunchaku by one stick, swung the other over his head and then forward with a whoosh, intending to break Rockson's cranium to shards.

Rockson brought his baton up. The steel rod, by the flick of a recessed button, suddenly exploded out from both ends, to three times its ten-inch length. The extended weapon met the nunchaku chain. The stick intended to smash Rock's skull swished by his nose several times in an instant. Rock had entangled the man's weapon for good.

Now Rockson, taking either end of the long baton in his steely grip, pulled with all the tensile strength his mutant muscles could deliver. He twisted to the side, yanked his attacker past him. Then Rock made him pay for his anger.

Any ordinary knife, even a huge bowie, would have been useless in this situation. The balisong, an ancient dual-handled butterfly knife of Filipino design, could be quickly drawn and opened. Rockson let go of one end of the baton, continuing to sweep his opponent past. Nunchaku-man wasn't bright enough

246

to let go of his now useless, entangled weapon and roll away. He struggled.

Rock used his free hand to pull the balisong from his belt crosshand, and with the same hand opened it.

Then he delivered the blade into the back of the man's skull, slicing into the spinal cord with a sickening snap, and twisting the thin cold blade. The blood ozzed out the open wound as the body sagged.

The cries of encouragement from the other two fighters became that of startled outrage now. One of their finest was gone within the flash of an eye. They could hardly believe it, judging from their wide eyes and their backing off a few feet.

Just enough pause in the action for Rockson to slip the baton from the nunchakus and get ahold of the dead enemy's weapon of choice.

Then the remaining two recovered from their shock.

"Lucky shot," Dedman snarled, sliding the gleaming broadsword from his scabbard, throwing his spear to the side. "Our friend was unaware you had the knife, and we're not."

"You're welcome to come and join him in hell," Rockson taunted. He smoothly snapped the butterfly knife's blade back into the handle and slipped it into his waistband. He swung his newly acquired nunchakas so rapidly the whooshing sound blotted out the shout of "*Killll*," that Dedman made as he charged at him.

Rockson's response was a fluid single movement, stepping to the side, dangling the nunchaku sticks at his side, redrawing his balisong from his waistband. Dedman wanted him to raise the sticks: the over-

247

whelming overhead swing of his massive weapon would meet the chain of Rockson's weapon and snap it and cut through the intruder's head.

But always do the unexpected, Chen had taught.

Rock kept the knife closed. He jabbed at his attacker's neck with the handle, smashing the blunt hardness inches deep in the pressure point exactly midway between the Adam's apple and the jugular vein of the swordsman as the blade clanked, sparks flying, against the hard floor tiles. Rockson did this maneuver instinctively, sensing rather than seeing where his opponent's neck was — a trick of ninjutsu he'd learned well from Chen.

It would have killed any normal man, but the peculiar exoskeletal structure of Dedman's mutated skeleton, just under his skin and thicker than normal, merely fractured. He rolled and stood up, screaming in pain, but he was alive.

And mad as hell.

It worked once, so why not again: "Here, piggy, piggy, piggy," Rock taunted. "Come to my slaughterhouse."

Dedman was wracked with pain; the blood from the blow that nearly had killed him coursed down his forehead, warm and sticky. But he had survived. And now he would change strategies, control his anger and attack a new way.

He shot an eye toward Bdos Err, who understood. Bdos had retrieved the spear and now he threw it to Dedman. Dedman caught it in his free hand and smiled crookedly — he only showed hints of emotion in battle, otherwise nothing *moved* him. Now, tasting

248

his own blood on his lips, he approached the strange man, the one who fought so unpredictably. Dedman got into a crouch. The sword . . . This time he would use a sideward swing, avoid the nunchaku the intruder was now swinging over his head. Avoid it by blocking it with the steel spear.

It was all over for the surface dweller.

Rockson threw the balisong with deadly accuracy. The blade stuck deep in the cruel heart of Dedman. The seven-inch blade, thrown with unerring accuracy, was so thin that it had done what Rock prayed it would do — split the bone shield under Dedman's slimy skin. And it had, sliding in to cut the aorta. The sword fell from the meaty hand that held it, clattering to the ground.

Dedman now lived up to his name.

"Sorry to be so unsportsmanlike," Rockson said, "but time is a-wasting."

One opponent now. The most deadly. Bdos circled to the left. He had his bullwhip out. The main event.

With a sinking heart, the Doomsday Warrior stood to face this challenge with the knowledge that it was probably too late to stop Stafford by now. At least two minutes had expired, enough time for Stafford to have escaped — with Factor Q. In just a few more minutes, he would make it to the probeshaft and fire it up to the surface.

Rockson shouted, "*Bdos*, here's a little knife for you too," and made like he was throwing something.

Bdos ducked the imaginary knife, shielding his eyes for a second — enough time for Rock to yank the balisong from its bloody home in Dedman's chest.

God, it was stuck in good. He barely made it.

Rock had grown attached to the slender weapon in this fight. It had accounted for two deaths, why not a third? As Chen stated often: *Always fight with the weapon you are most skilled with — if possible.*

But Rockson added, as he saw what was coming, *But don't get hung up on digging it out of a dead man.*

*SWWOOOOOOSSSSSHHHHHH.* The long lash of the bullwhip sailed out, and wrapped around Rock's legs so fast that he was spun off his feet and dragged across the floor in a mere fraction of a second. A second swoosh and a suprise shorter whip tore a red line across the Doomsday Warrior's back as he rolled, trying to unravel himself. The lash tore off his shirt.

Rock took advantage of his closeness to the attacker to jab with the balisong. He hit metal armor. *Shit.*

Rockson spun himself out of the grip of the bullwhip's cord before the second blow from the shorter whip struck.

He needed cover — and dove to get behind a cabinet. The whiplash came again, more accurately. The long leather cord sang through the air so quickly that Rockson was struck in middive. The long, snakelike thing caught him in the ankles and wrapped around them so tight that Rockson was stop-motioned and pulled down hard onto the floor. Bdos, with incredible strength, pulled the whip back toward him, with Rockson entrapped in its grip. Feet first, the Doomsday Warrior was headed toward death.

Using a ninja trick, making himself into a tight

ball, the axis of which was his imprisoned ankles, he spun ten times to the side like a whirlwind. He was free — for now.

He quickly recovered, snapped open his body, and leapt to the side — too late to avoid the tip of the long whipcord slashing a red gouge across his forehead. His eyes became obscured by blood. The whipcord's steel tip had missed them by mere inches. And then again, and again, the whip cracked the stillness. And Rockson rolled and rolled, like a mad dervish.

He found the baton. The whipcord sailed out again. Rock held the baton above his head.

The cord wrapped around the baton — and Rockson's wrist. The pain was intense. But he endured it. He held on as a mighty tug tried to free the whipcord. Blood pulsed out of torn cartilage on his wrist. Blood oozed down from his forehead into his eyes. The pain in a dozen parts of his steel-muscled bronze body was agonizing. But he held on. He had not only his own life at stake. The whole world depended on the next few seconds of this terror.

And Rockson, knowing the additional pain it would create, still forced himself to roll for his attacker, holding onto the long bullwhip cord.

*He had to get this over with.*

The smaller whip snapped out its message of ultimate pain, hitting the Doomsday Warrior in the groin. The blow was partly — but only partly — ameliorated by the metal zipper of his pants. The pain was unbearable yet had to be endured.

The shorter cord struck his face, slashing a gouge across his cheek. Dimly, through the blood in his bleary eyes, Rockson could see the look of triumph on Bdos Err's countenance.

Bdos struck again at Rock's face. And the Dooms-day Warrior, always unorthodox, snagged the second whipcord in his teeth, and bit hard onto it. He held on and got to his feet. Twisting like a top, he spun now, ramming his skull into the man's face.

His tormentor *oomphed* as his nose cracked, and as Rock raised his face before the man, he knew Bdos could take less pain than he could deliver. He was shaken.

Rock took the sheathed knife from Bdos Err's belt, used all his might to lift up one of Bdos Err's arms, and slammed the blade in toward the one spot on his massive chest area that the armor didn't cover—the space in the armor under the armpit. Pain drove him like no other incentive to destroy this man, this last fearsome obstacle to the pursuit of Stafford.

It was over, the look in his eyes told the story. Waning life. The strength of the man was sapped. Bdos Err, mightiest of Eden, was dying. And a gentleness came into his eyes.

He whispered as blood oozed from his lips. He uttered his last words: "I am loyal. All my life I have served the government . . ."

"Yes, you have," said Rockson, catching the sagging body, letting the weight of the man sag to the floor as the dark eyes rolled up.

"Yes, you have . . ."

252

# Chapter 28

Rockson thought that Stafford must be heading to the damned probe. The probe in the shaft that led to the surface. He was going to put the canister of ultimate death in the probe, fire it up to the surface. He had perhaps picked the moment when most of Eden slept to perpetrate this ultimate act of evil.

Rock checked the adjoining bedroom and another room, but he knew he would find no one. He was gone, and the means to destroy all life on Earth was with him.

Rockson ran back to the throne room. The Freefighters were all there, except for Archer. Archer soon appeared, dragging a senator by the scruff of his neck across the floor.

"Good work, Archer," Rockson said. Archer bowed, dropping the little frightened gray-robed man summarily in front of his big feet.

Upon sharp questioning, the senator stuttered out that the surface probe was at the far end of the Crypt Cave.

"The Crypt Cave is the burial palace of high officials. It is the closest place to the surface," Danik exclaimed.

"Let's go," Rock snapped out, "and burn down anyone that gets in our way."

Danik led them to the easternmost point of the city, just beyond the little metal "park." Rockson saw an archway with a lot of plastic flowers in pails on both sides of the portal.

"That's it," said Danik, breathing hard from the run — or the excitement.

Once inside the triangular door, Rockson and his team raced along between the marble sarcophagi, thousands of silent repositories for the people who never seen real sunlight or known love, for people who had lived and died in the stale atmosphere of this prison city.

Rockson soon was in the lead of all the Freefighters, and was first to plunge up the steeply inclined staircase that led to the probe shaft. There was a chance, he realized, making the fifth landing. Stafford was way out of shape; he probably was huffing and puffing not too far ahead. Rock stopped for an instant, and listened. Yes, labored footfalls, about three stories above. Madly he doubled-stepped the stairs, heading up with his burner at the ready. The lights on the stairs, bare bulbs connected by strings of wire tacked along the staircase ceiling, went out. He continued along the staircase in the darkness, feeling his way along the metal bannister.

Chen was, Rock surmised by the soft rapid footfalls, coming up behind him. The martial arts expert was swift in darkness, sensing rather than seeing where he was headed. Good, there might be a need for his hand-to-hand skills, especially if Stafford was armed and managed to kill Rock. Perhaps Chen could take over and save the day.

A flash of light seared the air, and Rock tumbled down a half flight to avoid it. A beam of heat from a disintegrator gun. He had caught up to Stafford. Now what?

There was silence. As he lay there, a hand touched Rockson's shoulder. Chen. Rock acknowledged the nudge. They were two against one now. But how could they press that advantage? Had Stafford reached the level where the probe was situated?

"Stop," Rockson yelled, "Let's talk, Stafford. *Don't do it*."

There was a high-pitched screech in the area above. What the hell? It wasn't a human scream. That came a moment later. There was the sound of leather snapping in the air; a wind coursed down the staircase.

The horrible human scream continued. Stafford's scream. There were flashbeams behind the two Freefighters, others of their company coming up the stairs. Danik was one of the first to reach them. "I heard," Danik gasped.

"Was it a giant bat?" Rock said. "How could it get in here?"

A trip to the top of the stairs showed how the seemingly impossible event had occurred.

"A tremor must have opened up the wall of this excavation to the cavern," Rock said as the flashbeams played around the ragged hole in the left wall of the small probe room.

Danik played his flashbeam around, finding the narrow shaftway that led upward, the missile-like surface probe still poised in it. Rockson rushed to the device and opened its compartment door. No Factor Q canister. So Stafford hadn't had time to put Factor Q into the missile. The bat had gotten Stafford first.

Rockson took up McCaughlin's electron binoculars and peered into the darkness of the cavern through the aperture in the wall. Desperately he adjusted the infrared power and the magnification to maximum, scanning the far reaches of the cavern—and saw a flapping thing, far away. A black shape. The bat, winging away with Stafford in its claws, heading away, away, down the long cavern corridors.

He put down the instrument. How was he to follow? And yet he must. He must be sure the canister was not burst open. Even if that happened in the depths of the cavern, the germs would spread slowly, make their way over time to the surface.

He pulled the powerful instrument from his eyes, and asked Danik for his flashlight. He played the light down into the cavern below them. He saw that the way was steep, but one could climb down. This he proceeded to do. He scrambled down the shifting sands of the underground embankment with no real plan in mind. He knew one thing, though. He had to retrieve that canister.

Once on the limestone floor below, Rockson considered waiting for his companions who were following, then changed his mind, plunging ahead at breakneck speed.

He ran for what seemed an hour but might have

been just a few minutes, then, exhausted, he fell heavily against a jutting rock formation. He was breathing heavily. It was silly, this running after a flying thing. A thing more powerful than a hundred men. A thing by now lost in the bowels of the Earth.

He let out a cry of utter hopelesssness.

Rockson's heart sank to its lowest level ever. All of his struggle, the immense trek, the terrible passage through the caverns of Eden, the death of Chief Smokestone—all for naught.

Surely the canister of death was shattered someplace in the cavern now, and slowly, inexorably, over the next few days the strange and deadly germ would permeate everywhere.

The glow of his flashlight annoyed him now, for he wanted the darkness to hide his tears. Rockson's flicked it off and wept alone in the darkness.

*Giggles*. The touch of icy thought fingers to his forehead. The damned Whisperers again, Rock thought, with anger. "*Go away*," Rockson shouted.

"Aren't you afraid of us?" the soft whisper said.

"What's to be afraid of?—the whole Earth is doomed."

"How so?" asked the gentle voice.

Rockson said, "Look. Whoever or whatever you are—you might as well know. I'm doomed, all is doomed. So leave me alone."

"I read into your thoughts. What you think is happening is horrible. It *must not be*. I must help you." There was a swishing sound, like the rippling of silk in the wind. A breeze caressed Rockson face.

And the voice was closer. "My name is Starlight.

Turn on your light and see me."

Curious and thinking to himself, Oh, why not, seeing this creature will fill in the last few hours of my life, Rockson turned on the light, and beheld a delightful girl child of about ten years of age — a girl dressed in a sparkling gossamer outfit, like a fairy. She had the softest blond hair and a cherubic face. She also had two green tendrils that looked like combed-back antennae on either side of her forehead. Telepathy apparatus.

# Chapter 29

"Starlight, can you really help?"

"I have powers, and friends. It is possible. I will call my great red friend." The child whistled long and slow. "There, that is done. Now while we wait — it will just be a moment — let me tell you about us Whisperers:

"We are the missing children of Eden. Our parents left us *hideous* children — we mutants look all scrunched up at birth — to die at the Sacrifice pool. They believed the cavern beings would take us and eat us. Many of the first to be abandoned died. Some among us crawled away and lived off the mushrooms — and survived. We took care of the others who were left at the waters after that. We are not as young as we look — we age very slowly. I am psychic, you are correct there — that is why I could immediately understand the peril. I know something good. The canister is yet intact."

There was the noise of a great flying thing swooping down from the cavern roof high above. Rock yelled, "*Down*," and went to draw his pistol.

"*No*," said the child. "It is only Ra-we-nak. The red bat. He is the friend I whistled for. He will help us find Stafford and retrieve the vial."

Rock flashed up his beam at the monstrous thing of leather wings that now swooped down and folded its wings. It waddled over to Starlight and nudged the girl child with its big single-horned head.

"Nice Ra-we-nak," Starlight said. "You must let us ride you; you must follow the vampire bat that has taken the man."

If a bat could look startled and uneasy, this one did. It shied away, trembled.

"Do not worry, Ra-we-nak," said Starlight. "We have a weapon, a heat pistol. And you must do this, so that we can all remain alive. Please. If you like me, and want me to be your friend anymore, please do this."

The creature's eyes became watery and it seemed to nod.

Rockson was prompted by Starlight to mount the giant flying steed. He shrugged, and holding the horn of the dark red saddle, he pulled himself up on the thing's back. This was all a hallucination anyway, he thought. One of the Whisperers' crazy mind-jokes. He'd go along for the ride.

Starlight climbed aboard, squeezing her cherubic little body in front of his. Then they took off at lightning speed, the giant red bat snapping its wings mightily to gain altitude.

It sure seemed real enough, Rockson thought,

hanging on for dear life as the floor of the cavern disappeared in the darkness.

Soon they were in a dull fiery red light. They were apparently going about a hundred miles an hour. Rock figured that from the flashing-past of a multitude of stalactites on either side of their flight path. They flew at the red glow in the distance. He felt like he was inside an intestine. And laughed. Perhaps this twisting huge tunnel was one of the bowels of the Earth. Ha ha, what an illusion.

And then he saw it—the huge black bat, floating along in front of them, holding Stafford's limp body in its claws. And Stafford's hand held a long slender cylinder. Factor Q.

# Chapter 30

Starlight exclaimed, "Yes, I see it too." The black bat didn't turn its prehistoric toothy head, but it must have sensed their approach, for it squawked and veered off, making a sound like a diving B-98 bomber. It dove down a corkscrewing fifty-meter-wide side tunnel.

"Hold on tight," Starlight said. Rockson dug his heels as hard as he could into the side of the giant red bat as it swung to the left and dropped like a meteor. Its wings had snapped shut, hurtling them down the precipitous side tunnel in pursuit of the black bat and its human prey. His stomach felt like it did in the high-speed elevator at Century City — queasy.

Ra-we-nak, their steedbat, snapped open its wings from time to time to change direction or make a sudden spin, following the spiraling near-vertical descent of the tunnel. It was gaining on the black bat, which took another wild turn down an even steeper pathway in the faintly luminous underground world.

As they continued plummeting downward, the

263

walls of the tunnel drew in tighter and tighter. Rockson could see it slipping by like the corrugated lining of some giant dark intestine at a mile a second. The red bat started screaming out a high-pitched sound, possibly to steer itself, listening to the echoes of its own shrill voice as a form of sonar. The Doomsday Warrior's ears hurt; he wished he could let go of Starlight and cover them, but it was too chancy.

They wove and spun, sometimes coming perilously close to a rocky wall of the corkscrewing tunnel. The air grew fetid and hot; the sulfurous smell increased. The Doomsday Warrior's ears popped again and again as the pressure increased.

God, if this kept up, he thought, they would soon reach the flaming hot magma lying miles under the Earth's crust.

"Starlight," Rock shouted, "where are we going?"

"To hell itself — where the dark creature, the ruler of all the vampire bats, nests."

The bomber-sized black bat disappeared from view momentarily around a sharp corner, then reappeared. They were gaining on it. Rockson's wind-teared eyes squinted over the red bat's head to see that Stafford was still held in the grip of the thing — and the canister was still in his death grip.

As the suffocating, sulfurous-smelling high-pressure winds whipped by, the noise his steed's leathery wings made mimicked a Stuka dive bomber. The yawing and rolling of their impossible flight path through volcanic tunnels deep under the Earth continued until Rock felt his ears would burst. He was near to blacking out.

Gravity ceased to have any meaning. They were

upside down, then upright, then upside down again. The Doomsday Warrior jammed his heels in against the stiff body of his unearthly mount, wishing he had stirrups, holding on for dear life, his arms locked around the small soft body of Starlight.

How far had they come in the five minutes of flight in the glowing red dimness? It seemed like a thousand miles. They were somewhere deep into the Earth's bowels. It was growing very hot — perhaps they neared the source of the volcanic light.

Now they came out in a large cavern lit by the orange glow of a flowing river of red hot lava. They leveled off, rode through thunder and lightning, swirling clouds of blue and gray smoke. The killer bat was less than a hundred meters ahead. Ninety, eighty . . . and slowing.

And then they lost it. Their red bat screeched and screeched, trying to get an echo from the big killer, but to no avail. There was too much thunderous electrical display all around.

Rockson asked that they fly in a search pattern, over the fiery stream of lava, where the clouds were less thick.

Rock scanned the cavern as they traveled, soaring in large arcs, as he had indicated to Starlight.

Starlight shouted, "There it is," pointing over to the right. At the far end of the chamber, high on a ledge, was a nest — but not a bird's nest of straw. This nest was of metal — pipes and gears and other man-made things plucked from the area near Eden and flown here, then woven and bent into the giant vampire bat's nest.

And perched in that nest of twisted metal pipes on

the far ledge above the red flowing river of lava was the vampire bat — and Stafford.

Stafford was torn open. Obviously dead. The canister containing Factor Q was nowhere to be seen.

The giant black bat was preoccupied, too preoccupied to notice the approaching red bat and its human cargo. The vampire bat had the man's carcass in its beak and was shaking it, dribbling its blood into the jaws of its three hellish bat-chicks.

Rockson had his shotpistol up; they approached at enormous speed. "I have to see if the canister is in the nest — attact its attention with a near pass. Get it to follow us."

Starlight whispered something into their mount's ear and the red bat began screeching an angry attack litany. Now the creature of darkness shifted and dropped the human body alongside the bat-chicks. Rockson could hear the three smaller black bats screech for their supper, angry that they had been cut off from the warm blood feast. The mother bat shifted and took to the air.

Rockson saw the canister teeter-tottering on the edge of the nest where it had lodged. If it fell from its current position, it would drop a few hundred feet and hit sharp rocks. And probably crack open, releasing its death to the world.

But if the canister could be dropped in the fiery lava river it would be instantly vaporized. Cleansed. Destroyed.

The red bat swung into a long arc of escape as the black mother bat followed, shrieking. It wanted to drive them from the area of its offspring. Motherly instinct — even in hell itself.

Rockson shouted, "Lose it in the smoke clouds, then get back to the nest and get that canister. Drop it in the lake of fire."

Easier said than done. The black bat was as tenacious as a fighter pilot following a target drone. Finally they lost it, and doubled back to the nest. Rockson could hardly bear to look as they came out of the clouds of steam and sulfur. But to his relief, the canister was still on the edge of the nest, jammed between two pipes — for now.

"Dive in, get the canister, drop it in the lava," Rock screamed.

The red bat dove, and at that moment the black bat swooped out of the clouds and screeched a horrible challenge. It probably meant something like "Don't get near my kids," and Rockson knew it meant it.

"Get the canister," he shouted.

He started firing his weapon over his shoulder, aiming for the fierce orange-glowing eyes of the nest defender. He really didn't expect to kill the thing — God knew how many shots that would take, even point-blank — or if it were possible at all. But he hoped to slow the attack enough for their own bat to snatch the canister up.

The vampire bat was hit, the X-pattern shots from his pistol smashing fist-sized holes into the thick skin of the flying creature. It veered off, screaming a different tune, its mouth dripping blood.

Ra-we-nak's claws scratched the canister as it flashed by the nest, but only succeeded in dislodging it. The canister careened down toward the jagged rocks far below.

"Catch it, catch it," Rock yelled, and the bat dove with all the power at its disposal.

It would be close. And no second tries this time.

"Please God, please," Rock begged the Almighty. "Please let it be caught."

Willy Mays couldn't have made a better save-the-game catch. Ra-we-nak's left claw closed around the canister just a foot from the jagged rocks, and majestically pulled out of the power dive, narrowly missing dousing itself—and its riders—in the smoldering lake of fire.

"Drop it in the fire," Rock yelled triumphantly.

This the red bat did with a flair, screeching what must have been a victory song. Rock saw the canister of Factor Q hit the lava, spark briefly, and then sink. A few seconds later there was a bubbling at the surface. Then nothing.

"Let's head home," Rockson said, heaving a sigh of relief. Now all Rockson had to do was get his people back to the surface, and trek a thousand frozen miles back to Century City.

He'd find a way. After all, he was the Doomsday Warrior.

# ACTION ADVENTURE

**SILENT WARRIORS**                                (1675, $3.95)
by Richard P. Henrick
*The Red Star*, Russia's newest, most technologically advanced
submarine, outclasses anything in the U.S. fleet. But when the
captain opens his sealed orders 24 hours early, he's staggered to
read that he's to spearhead a massive nuclear first strike against
the Americans!

**THE PHOENIX ODYSSEY**                            (1789, $3.95)
by Richard P. Henrick
All communications to the USS *Phoenix* suddenly and mysteri-
ously vanish. Even the urgent message from the president cancel-
ling the War Alert is not received. In six short hours the *Phoenix*
will unleash its nuclear arsenal against the Russian mainland.

**COUNTERFORCE**                                   (2013, $3.95)
Richard P. Henrick
In the silent deep, the chase is on to save a world from destruction. A single Russian Sub moves on a silent and sinister course
for American shores. The men aboard the U.S.S. *Triton* must
search for and destroy the Soviet killer Sub as an unsuspecting
world races for the apocalypse.

**EAGLE DOWN**                                     (1644, $3.75)
by William Mason
To western eyes, the Russian Bear appears to be in hibernation —
but half a world away, a plot is unfolding that will unleash it awesome, deadly power. When the Russian Bear rises up, God help
the Eagle.

**THE OASIS PROJECT**                              (1296, $3.50)
by William Mason
The President had a plan — a plan that by all rights should not
exist. And it would be carried out by the ASP, a second generation space shuttle that would transport the laser weapons into positions — before the Red Tide hit U.S. shores.

*Available wherever paperbacks are sold, or order direct from the
Publisher. Send cover price plus 50¢ per copy for mailing and
handling to Zebra Books, Dept. 2098, 475 Park Avenue South,
New York, N.Y. 10016. Residents of New York, New Jersey and
Pennsylvania must include sales tax. DO NOT SEND CASH.*

## THE WORLD-AT-WAR SERIES
### by Lawrence Cortesi

**COUNTDOWN TO PARIS**                    (1548, $3.25)
Having stormed the beaches of Normandy, every GI had one
dream: to liberate Paris from the Nazis. Trapping the enemy in
the Falaise Pocket, the Allies would shatter the powerful German
7th Army Group, opening the way for the . . . COUNTDOWN
TO PARIS.

**GATEWAY TO VICTORY**                    (1496, $3.25)
After Leyte, the U.S. Navy was at the threshold of Japan's Pacific
Empire. With his legendary cunning, Admiral Halsey devised a
brilliant plan to deal a crippling blow in the South China Sea to
Japan's military might.

**ROMMEL'S LAST STAND**                    (1415, $3.25)
In April of 1943 the Nazis attempted a daring airlift of supplies
to a desperate Rommel in North Africa. But the Allies were lying
in wait for one of the most astonishing and bloody air victories of
the war.

**LAST BRIDGE TO VICTORY**                    (1393, $3.25)
Nazi troops had blown every bridge on the Rhine, stalling
Eisenhower's drive for victory. In one final blood-soaked battle,
the fanatic resistance of the Nazis would test the courage of every
American soldier.

**PACIFIC SIEGE**                    (1363, $3.25)
If the Allies failed to hold New Guinea, the entire Pacific would
fall to the Japanese juggernaut. For six brutal months they
drenched the New Guinea jungles with their blood, hoping to live
to see the end of the . . . PACIFIC SIEGE.

**THE BATTLE FOR MANILA**                    (1334, $3.25)
A Japanese commander's decision—against orders—to defend
Manila to the death led to the most brutal combat of the entire
Pacific campaign. A living hell that was . . . THE BATTLE FOR
MANILA.

*Available wherever paperbacks are sold, or order direct from the
Publisher. Send cover price plus 50¢ per copy for mailing and
handling to Zebra Books, Dept. 2098, 475 Park Avenue South,
New York, N.Y. 10016. Residents of New York, New Jersey and
Pennsylvania must include sales tax. DO NOT SEND CASH.*